THIRTEEN

THE SOC13TY OF THIRTEEN

GARETH P. JONES

First published in Great Britain in 2013 by Hot Key Books
Northburgh House, 10 Northburgh Street, London EC1V 0AT

A CIP catalogue record for this book is available from the British Library.

ISBN: 978-1-4714-0055-1

1

This book is typeset in 11pt Sabon

Printed and bound by Clays Ltd, St Ives Plc

Hot Key Books supports the Forest Stewardship Council (FSC), the leading international forest certification organisation, and is committed to printing only on Greenpeace-approved FSC-certified paper.

www.hotkeybooks.com

Hot Key Books is part of the Bonnier Publishing Group
www.bonnierpublishing.com

To my wonderful wife, Lisa, who brings magic into my life

Prologue

Amy clambers over the wall and drops into the cemetery. It's ridiculous that they lock the gates at night. Who would want to enter a cemetery after dark? Even Amy understands it isn't exactly normal. The lady who comes on Wednesdays doesn't like the word 'normal'. She says that everyone has their own idea of normality.

Amy has lived with her grandparents since the death of her mother, but they don't know about her visits to the cemetery. Tonight she snuck out unseen while they were watching television. They think it is she who is lost in an imaginary world, but her characters are more real than those miserable soap people. At least hers were alive.

The names on the gravestones now populate the story she is writing but they once had real lives. Amy has researched them as best she can. Sir Augustus Tyrrell was a politician. Mr G. Hayman was an American novelist, who wrote stories about magic, whereas Mr John Symmonds wrote dull-sounding books with long titles about language and grammar. Harry Clay was a famous illusionist and the only one of her characters who doesn't share their year of death: 1891.

The lady who comes on Wednesdays asks lots of questions about Amy's story, because she thinks it will reveal clues about what's wrong with her. Amy can tell she thinks she's weird, even if she wouldn't ever use that word. Most thirteen-year-old girls have friends. They don't have such difficulty talking to others. They don't feel as though sometimes the world is collapsing in on them. They aren't forced to see people like the lady who comes on Wednesdays. They don't spend their time making up long, complicated stories, filled with names plucked off gravestones.

Amy likes it here in her imagination and here in the cemetery. Other people would probably be scared somewhere so spooky so late at night. They would worry about ghosts or muggers or worse. Amy doesn't believe in ghosts. And what mugger would be stupid enough to hang around a place no one in their right mind would go? As for the worse, they are already present in Amy's imaginary world.

Under a weeping willow, Amy finds her favourite gravestone. The words have been worn away over the years, but they are still just about visible. Amy uses her torch to find the name of the character her story begins with: *Lord Silas Ringmore*.

A breeze chills Amy's bones. She rubs her arms to warm herself. Something moves in the bushes. Amy tells herself not to be scared. She wouldn't be scared if she heard the same noise during the day, but the darkness does strange things to the imagination.

Something rustles again. Amy picks up a stick to defend herself with in case it does turn out to be a murderer or a mugger, or something worse.

London, 1891

I

Ringmore

The Magnificent Meze had them in the palm of his hand. For the last hour, this mysterious, dark-skinned gentleman, clad in a flowing robe and speaking with an exotic accent, had captivated the packed audience of the London theatre. They had watched wide-eyed as he summoned dark forces to lift a series of objects from a table on one side of the stage then transport them across to another. They had witnessed him slice his beautiful assistant in two then reconnect both halves, apparently causing no harm to the lady. The grand finale had involved a volunteer from the second row, who was made to vanish from inside a cabinet on the stage then reappear in one of the royal boxes. As the volunteer stepped out, looking utterly bewildered, the applause was as thunderous as the grand old theatre had ever heard. The Magnificent Meze raised his hands and threw back his head, soaking up the adulation.

'Thank you for your generous applause. I hope you have

been entertained this evening,' he said once the applause died away. 'But more importantly, I hope that I have shown you that the universe contains a great many aspects beyond your understanding. The study of spiritualism and mysticism has much to tell us about the world, but tonight I speak to you of the elements which I have harnessed for this performance. The unseen elements which surround us . . .' He lowered his voice to a whisper. 'I speak to you of magic.'

The silence that followed was pierced by a singular utterance from a voice in the stalls. 'Balderdash.'

A look of puzzlement crossed the magician's face. 'Who speaks this word?'

In contrast to the magician's colourful attire, the man who stood up was dressed entirely in black, from the tips of his expensive shoes to the top of his pristine top hat.

'Let us have the house lights, please,' spoke the Magnificent Meze. 'I would like to see this naysayer.'

The lights came on to reveal the gentleman's face. He had angular cheekbones, a pointed nose and piercing eyes. His right hand rested lightly on the ornate golden handle of a black walking stick.

'You will have to forgive me,' said the Magnificent Meze. 'I have not long been in your country. I am not familiar with some of your words. Please explain this word, *balderdash*.'

'Certainly,' replied the man. 'It means piffle, nonsense . . . lies.'

'You are accusing me of being a liar?'

'I am, sir.'

'I consider this a great insult.'

'Then it seems you understand me perfectly.'

A titter spread through the audience as they realised they were to get yet more drama for no extra cost. This was better than an encore.

The Magnificent Meze looked less impressed by the interruption. 'You have not been entertained this evening?' he said.

'Entertained? Certainly,' said the man. 'But your suggestion that there is any more to this spectacular evening's entertainment than stage trickery is pure deceit. Retract this claim and I will not embarrass you by revealing your methods.'

'I will do nothing of the kind,' replied the Magnificent Meze. 'I have already revealed my methods. Magic, which was once commonly used, has become the stuff of myths and stories, but I harness the very real threads of magic which hold together our world and weave them into the performances you have witnessed.'

'Very well.' The man stepped out into the aisle and walked briskly towards the stage, stick in hand, before leaping up into the limelight.

The Magnificent Meze looked decidedly put out by the man's appearance. 'In my country, such interruptions are not usual.'

'Then welcome to England,' replied the gentleman, 'the land of the cynic.'

'Who are you?'

'My name is Lord Ringmore and I am here to tear through

the fabric of your lies.' He looked up. 'Yes, as I thought, there is plenty of room up there for your stage hands to lift the objects with wires, unseen in the dim lighting required to conjure these mischievous spirits of yours.'

'I object –' began the magician.

Lord Ringmore interrupted him. 'You employ as much magic as a fisherman uses to catch fish.'

The Magnificent Meze's obvious annoyance was only increased by the laughter from the audience. Lord Ringmore marched to the back of the stage and wheeled out the box, inside which the girl had been halved.

'Ladies and gentlemen,' he said. 'Up close, it is clear that this box is large enough to contain two women, each tucked up in their own compartments. While we saw the head of the pretty assistant, the lovely legs belonged to a second woman. A smoothly executed trick, I'll grant you, but nothing supernatural.'

'Who are you that would stand here and denounce the magic to which I have dedicated my life?' cried the Magnificent Meze.

'I am one who has dedicated his life to the search for real magic. I came here in search of it. Sadly, all I have seen are cheap tricks carried out with confident bombast and overblown theatrical flair. Do you really want me to continue with this dissection?'

'Your explanations are little more than conjecture,' replied the Magnificent Meze. 'Did you not just witness me transport a man from this stage across the theatre? How do you explain that?'

Lord Ringmore tapped the stage with his stick. 'The man was hidden inside the cabinet. The trapdoor opened, allowing him to drop below the stage. Then, while you regaled the audience with your lengthy and entirely nonsensical dissection of the mechanics of magic, he hurriedly made his way to the box, which was conveniently empty. Surprising, since tonight's performance was sold out.'

'In which case, would this man not be aware of his involvement?' The Magnificent Meze turned to the volunteer, now back in his seat. 'Sir,' he said. 'Is this true? Let me remind the audience that, before this evening, we had never met.'

The volunteer stood. 'I don't know nothing about no trapdoor,' he said. 'All I know is that one minute I was standing on the stage, the next, I was in that box. I don't know what this fella's on about. What I experienced tonight will haunt me till my dying day. My dying day, I say . . .'

Lord Ringmore smiled. 'May I ask your name, sir?'

'Er, Bill,' replied the man.

'Your full name, if you would be so kind.'

'William Maybury.'

'Maybury,' repeated Lord Ringmore. He looked at the Magnificent Meze then back to the man in the stalls, demonstrating a certain flair for performance himself. 'Maybury,' he said again, rolling the word in his mouth. 'It's the strangest thing. Now I come to look at the two of you, I have to confess I see a certain resemblance.'

The Magnificent Meze laughed. 'I would say the differences were more obvious than the similarities. Except, of course, that we are all God's children.'

'Very true,' said Lord Ringmore. 'Remind me where you come from?'

'I was born in the ancient, mystical city of Baghdad.'

'Ah, yes. I have travelled extensively myself. I spent a month in your beautiful home city. I found the view afforded from the Mountain of Osmagog most breathtaking.'

'It is indeed beautiful,' said the Magnificent Meze, bowing graciously.

'There is no such place,' snapped Lord Ringmore. 'And I fear your complexion owes more to the generous application of boot polish than to your mother's colouring. In fact, now that I see you up close, I fear the stuff is rubbing off around your collar.' He turned to the audience. 'This evening you have been entertained not by a mystical medium called Meze, but by a two-bit performer called Maybury. David and William Maybury, a pair of brothers, married to the top and bottom half of the poor bisected woman whom you so enjoyed watching being halved this evening.'

'Why, you rotten little . . .' began the Magnificent Meze, dropping his accent. Seeing him approach with raised fists, Lord Ringmore stepped back and, with one swift movement, banged on a floorboard. A trapdoor below the Magnificent Meze immediately opened and the stage suddenly swallowed him up.

The audience gasped as though it was witnessing the final act of a play.

'Ladies and gentlemen,' said Lord Ringmore, 'I hope you have enjoyed this evening's performance. Personally, I hold the skill involved in these public deceptions in the utmost regard but please be under no misapprehension: nothing you have witnessed this evening owes the slightest thing to real magic.'

Perhaps deciding that this interruption was in fact a well-orchestrated part of the show after all, the audience marked Lord Ringmore's exit with one final appreciative round of applause.

2

Book

Lord Ringmore had to admit that the Maybury brothers had executed their act with slick professionalism, even keeping the Magnificent Meze's London debut shrouded in enticing secrecy before the opening night. Until he had set eyes on the boot-polished face of David Maybury, Lord Ringmore had allowed himself to believe that this could be the one. More than anything he longed to witness a trick that could not be explained. He stepped out of the theatre into the busy London thoroughfare having had his expectations shattered.

On the street corner an impassioned evangelist railed against the sins so readily available in the city. Lord Ringmore envied the certainty with which he spoke of God's judgement. As a young man, following the loss of his parents, Silas Ringmore had been a regular churchgoer. No one prayed as fervently, nor sang as loudly as he but, as he grew from lonely child to lonely man, the itching doubt in his heart grew. He became restless. He traversed countries and continents, dabbling with every religion and belief system he found, just as a man might try on different styles of clothing. But too often, he found corruption and self-interest far too prevalent and divine intervention distinctly absent. The world's religions would not help him find that which he sought.

Lord Ringmore crossed the road to avoid the evangelist's fevered ranting and heard another voice speaking his name.

'Excuse me, Lord Ringmore?'

Lord Ringmore tightened his grip on the walking stick. Although he carried it as an affectation, it did occasionally serve as an excellent weapon to ward off London's countless beggars. However, the owner of the voice did not look like a beggar. He wore a brown suit and cloth cap, which he doffed respectfully when Lord Ringmore turned to face him.

'What do you want?' demanded Lord Ringmore.

'My question is *what do you want?*' replied the man. 'And once we have established that we must, as inhabitants of a mercurial world, ask how much you will pay for it?'

'You were in the theatre?' Lord Ringmore sighed.

'I was.'

'Then you'll understand two things about me. Firstly, I do not suffer fools gladly. Secondly, I possess a stick, with which you run a severe risk of being beaten unless you come to the point presently.'

It was not the first time someone had learnt of Lord Ringmore's interest and set out to take advantage of it.

'You seek the truth,' said the man. 'The truth about magic.'

'I swear, if you pull a pack of cards from your pocket you will not sit down comfortably for a week,' replied Lord Ringmore.

'I am no magician,' said the man.

'Then what, pray, are you?'

'I was a shop owner until my shop was burnt to the ground, with everything in it.'

'So you are a salesman with nothing to sell.'

'I do have one thing to sell. It is an object that I believe will be of great interest to you.' The man lowered his voice. 'It is a magical object.'

'What kind of magical object?'

'A book.'

'I see. You are not a magician and yet you have a magic book. Allow me to guess. Would it be a book of spells?'

'I do not know, for it is written in a language that I cannot read, if it is a language at all.'

'And how much are you asking for this incomprehensible book?'

'I will lend you the book for one night and if you are not satisfied by morning that it is the genuine article then I will take it from you and ask no payment.'

Lord Ringmore was intrigued. If this was trickery then it was, at least, an original trick. 'Let me see this object,' he said.

The man pulled out a small black book. On the back, drawn in white, was a circle within a triangle within a circle.

On the front, embossed in faded gold, was the number thirteen. Lord Ringmore took it and ran his fingers over the cover. He opened it and looked at a page. The rough paper was covered in patterns similar to those on the back cover.

'What use is an unreadable book?' asked Lord Ringmore.

'It will not be the reading of it that proves its authenticity,' replied the man. 'I will name my price tomorrow. You can decide then whether you are willing to pay for it.'

Lord Ringmore pocketed the book and felt a familiar fluttering of his heart. In the theatre he had used the word 'cynic', but that was inaccurate. A cynic would never feel such hope. Lord Ringmore was often disappointed by a cynical world, but he was, at heart, a romantic. He was a believer.

3

Orphans

A close observer would have noticed a bounce in Lord Ringmore's purposeful stride as he crossed Golden Square. He was excited. He was enjoying the rhythmical click of his walking stick as he approached his club. He would dine there alone tonight. He was not yet ready for company. He needed to decide on a course of action before he spoke to anyone else.

'Excuse me, mister.'

The child's voice, though quiet, was loud enough to snap him out of his thoughts. He turned to see a young boy who seemed no older than twelve or thirteen years, although malnourishment and hard living made it difficult to tell with street children. His dark hair was unwashed and matted. His clothes were ragged.

Lord Ringmore raised his stick. 'I will give you a moment to consider whether your begging will be worth the beating I am about to administer.'

'Sorry, mister. I ain't no beggar though. It's just I think you dropped this.'

In his grubby hand, the boy held a shilling. Lord Ringmore tapped his pockets.

'Are you sure it's mine?' he asked.

'I was just standing there, sir, by that bench when I saw something fall from your coat. I raced over and found this shilling, so I'm as sure as I can be.'

Lord Ringmore took the shilling from the boy's hand. 'A very honest young lad you are,' he said, pocketing the coin.

'Thank you, sir,' said the boy.

'But if you are expecting some reward for doing your honest duty as a citizen I'm afraid you are in for severe disappointment,' said Lord Ringmore.

'Good acts are their own reward,' said the boy. 'That's what the nuns taught us at the orphanage.'

'They are right,' said Lord Ringmore. He reached into his pocket for a penny to throw the boy but, as he did so, he felt a slight tug on his coat. He spun around to find a girl with her hand deep in his other coat pocket. Quick as a flash, he grabbed her wrist. The boy made to escape but Lord Ringmore issued a sharp whack with his stick to the boy's shins then let the stick fall to the ground and took hold of his skinny arm.

'So that's your game, is it?' he snarled, dragging the two children around so that they both faced him. 'A pair of thieves, eh?'

'Let go!' said the boy.

'Please sir, it's only hunger what made us do it,' pleaded

the girl. She looked the same age as the boy. They both had grubby faces but the girl had been blessed with light brown eyes that shone out like pennies in the dirt.

'A neat little scheme you have going here,' continued Lord Ringmore. 'The boy plays the part of a good Samaritan, lowering your victim's defences. While you engage the victim's attention, this girl fleeces your mark for everything he's got, including the shilling which you used to set up the scenario. But I'm afraid you picked the wrong target this evening.' Noticing a policeman walking through the square, his hands behind his back, Lord Ringmore cried, 'Officer! Your assistance, please.'

The policeman raised a hand in acknowledgement and walked briskly to join them.

'Please don't,' said the boy.

'Yes, please, sir, our mother lies on her deathbed,' said the girl. 'We only take so that we can buy enough to keep her alive.'

'Poor Ma,' said the boy. 'She would die of shame to see us thieving, but what else can we do?'

Both children burst into tears and were sobbing uncontrollably when the policeman arrived.

'These two urchins pickpocketing, were they?' asked the officer. 'Don't you worry, sir, I know how to deal with filthy little thieving rats like them.'

The commotion had also drawn the attention of a large woman carrying a small dog, who had raced over to join in the drama. 'I saw the whole thing, officer,' she said. 'No one is safe while such guttersnipes plague our streets. They need to be locked up, punished.'

'I'll see to that,' said the officer. 'I can take it from here, sir.'

'I'm sorry, officer,' said Lord Ringmore. 'I'm afraid I have misled you. You see, these two work for me. They were misbehaving, so I called you over to scare them and bring them into line. As you can see, it has had the desired effect. They won't play me up again, will you?'

The two children shook their heads, still in tears.

'But I saw the girl reach into your pocket . . .' stated the woman with the dog. 'I saw her.'

'While I thank you for your interest I can assure you these children are no more thieves than I am,' said Lord Ringmore. 'I'm very sorry to have wasted your time, officer, but I thank you for your quick assistance. You are doing a fine job. I, for one, feel heartened by the speed of your response.'

'So long as you are absolutely certain,' said the officer.

'I couldn't be more so.'

'Well, I'm sure I've never seen such behaviour,' said the woman, but she and the policeman left Lord Ringmore and the two orphans.

Once they had gone, both children stopped crying, sniffed and looked up at Lord Ringmore. 'Thank you, sir. Our poor ma . . .'

'Orphans with a mother?' said Lord Ringmore. 'That is original. Please don't insult me further by continuing with your dying mother story. It has even less credence than the dropped shilling scam.'

Neither child spoke.

'You have been spared the punishment of the law on one condition,' said Lord Ringmore. 'As I just told that officer, you work for me now.'

'Work for you?' said the girl.

'Precisely. Now, please furnish me with your names.'

'Tom and Esther,' said the boy.

'You are not brother and sister,' said Lord Ringmore emphatically. 'Can you read?'

'They taught us our numbers and letters at the orphanage sir, but neither of us can read well,' said the girl.

'But you can read addresses? And you know London, yes?'

'Yes, sir.'

'Good.' Lord Ringmore released the children and retrieved his walking stick from the ground. 'Now, before I give you the details of your duties and we find more suitable clothing for you –'

'What's wrong with our clothes?' interrupted Tom.

'If you are to work for me you will need to be smarter and less . . . aromatic. But before we begin, I think we should establish what I will call a contract of mistrust. Esther, if you would be so kind as to return my wallet that you snatched just then as I bent to pick up my stick.'

Esther glanced at Tom then sulkily handed the wallet back to Lord Ringmore.

'You have commendable sleight of hand,' said Lord Ringmore. 'Perhaps one day you will make better use of it but for now you'll have to settle for a more mundane occupation.'

'What occupation?' asked Tom.

'I need you both to act as my discreet messengers,' said Lord Ringmore.

4

Trust

'I don't like it. Not one bit,' said Tom. 'A top-hatted toff like that offering us work when he knows full well we tried to take from him? I don't trust him.'

'You don't trust anyone,' said Esther.

'We can't afford trust,' said Tom.

Tom and Esther were sitting in an upstairs room of a decrepit warehouse overlooking the river. Since abandoning St Clement's Catholic School for Waifs and Strays in favour of life on the streets it was the closest thing they had to a home. They had found the place when on the run from a stall-owner at Rotherhithe market. The warehouse was in such a sorry state that there was no staircase inside, but Tom, the better climber of the two, had found a way up and round the outside to the room upstairs. It was a dangerous climb. One slip and they would end up in the Thames, but the difficulty made it a safer place to spend their nights.

The warehouse was the orphans' current favourite hide-spot but they knew it wouldn't last for long. Sooner or later they would be discovered, or someone would come to knock down the building. It had happened before and it was only a matter of time before it happened again. Esther had even come up with the idea of lighting a fire on the north bank of the river as a signal if one of them needed to warn the other that it was time to get out. Then they would move on to some other forgotten corner of London. There were always more places to hide.

Esther emptied her pockets of the day's takings onto her mattress. There wasn't much and they were all objects that would need to be sold on. She sat down and looked out at the fast-flowing river.

'If we don't work for him he'll have us sent down,' she said.

'London ain't exactly a village,' said Tom. 'All we have to do is avoid being seen by him again. Ain't so difficult. It's not like we work that part of town much anyhow. I told you it was risky over there. Did you see how quickly that copper appeared?'

'So we stay away from Piccadilly too now, do we?' said Esther. 'We'll be avoiding half of the city at this rate. What if this Ringmore job means a chance to stop thieving?'

'You really want to run messages for that old toff?'

'Why not?'

'Who knows what else he'll have us doing? He looks like the sort that's wrong in the head if you ask me. What if he locks us in a cage and murders us?'

Esther sighed. 'He's moneyed and he's offering us honest work.'

'How do you know it's honest?' asked Tom. 'I mean, who in their right mind would want us working for them?'

Esther laughed in spite of herself. 'I agree that this ain't what we're used to, but what we're used to ain't exactly tea at the palace. All I'm saying is, who cares what he's up to so long as we stand to gain from it?'

'What we gaining?' demanded Tom, picking up a piece of rubble from the floor and hurling it out of the broken window into the Thames. 'A couple of coins that we could make in an afternoon? You should have been quicker emptying his pockets. I did my part well enough.'

Esther stood up angrily. 'I was quick. It's more likely he saw through your act.'

'He certainly didn't fall for that poor dying ma business, that's for sure.'

'We'll go back and see him tomorrow as we said,' said Esther. 'We'll do this work for him. Maybe something will come of it. Maybe not. But there's no harm in trying.'

'I'd rather throw my lot in with Hardy than deliver messages for him,' said Tom, sulkily.

'We agreed we ain't never working for Hardy,' said Esther.

'Come on, Est,' said Tom, sitting back down. 'You know the way things are going. We can't keep running and hiding from him.'

'What you saying, Tom?'

'I'm saying maybe Hardy ain't so bad. The others seem to be getting on all right. Maybe we should do a deal.'

'No. You know how I feel about him,' said Esther. 'I'd rather die than work for that rogue.'

'That might be the choice we've got.'

'Please Tom. Give this a chance. Perhaps Hardy will lay off us if he sees we've got a job . . . a *real* job, I mean, working for a gentleman like Ringmore.'

Tom pulled a bruised apple from his pocket. 'Perhaps,' he said. He sunk his teeth into the apple.

'I don't think we can carry on like this forever,' said Esther.

'Who cares about forever?' asked Tom. 'It's what we do now that matters.'

'And I say that we try this out now. At least we'll get some new clothes out of it.'

'New clothes don't matter if you're murdered and locked in a cage,' said Tom.

'Being locked in a cage don't matter if you're murdered.'

Tom laughed. 'Oh, all right – but don't say I didn't warn you.'

5

Politics

As far as the Right Honourable Sir Augustus Tyrrell MP was concerned there was very little more irksome than having to spend time with one's constituents. Now he was a prominent member of the cabinet he didn't have time for such things, but even with his safe Tory seat, it was sometimes advisable to show his face at these public forums. There was a groundswell of worryingly liberal ideas that required quashing. The natural order of things was in jeopardy. The Labour movement and the trade unions were bad enough, but votes for women? It was clearly a joke, and yet the levity with which he had tackled the subject had incensed the woman in the front row of this draughty town hall.

'My dear lady,' Sir Tyrrell said. 'You have had your say. Now, please allow me mine.'

'You have had your say for over two thousand years,' replied the woman.

'Do I really look that old?' he replied, raising his eyebrows and playing the crowd.

Laughter was an MP's greatest ally in a public forum. Get them laughing and you have them on your side.

'You know full well that I am talking about men,' said the woman, undeterred.

'Forgive me, I thought we were discussing precisely the opposite,' he said, soaking up yet more approving mirth. He wondered if this woman's poor husband knew she was here making a fool of herself.

'Increasing numbers of women have jobs,' said the woman. 'They mother their children and, more often than not, their husbands. Why should they not have a say in who rules them?'

Sir Tyrrell smiled. 'You think running a household is the same as running the country?'

'I don't think it so very different,' she replied. 'One must balance the books, hire and fire staff, ensure the well-being of the household.'

'And because you women are burdened with such things, why not leave the complex business of politics and economics to your husbands? It seems to me a perfect way to share the load of life.'

'I believe you are frightened, sir,' she said.

'Frightened of *women*?' said Sir Tyrrell, gaining not quite as much of a laugh as he had hoped. Perhaps the audience could tell from his tone that there was some truth in her assertion. The most prominent female figures in his life had been his mother and his nanny, both utterly ferocious women. Apart from that, his only experience of the so-called fairer sex was a small army of sour-faced aunts who had plagued his youth by trying and failing to find him a suitable partner. As his waistline and complexion revealed, Sir Tyrrell had more of a taste for fine dining and expensive brandy than for matters of the heart. 'I'm afraid it's precisely this kind of hysterical outburst which proves my point,' he pronounced.

'Hear, hear,' cried various male voices.

'Leave it to the men,' shouted one.

'Sit down, woman. You're embarrassing yourself,' added another.

Sir Tyrrell continued. 'Women do not have access to the clear logic and rational thought required for important decision making.'

The round of applause was music to his ears.

'I do not need a lecture on rationality from a man who spends his time delving into the occult,' said the tenacious woman.

'It sounds to me as though that is exactly what you need,' said Sir Tyrrell, standing up and adopting his most statesman-like pose, with his thumbs resting in his waistcoat. 'I have never hidden my interest in the occult. I am not ashamed of it. It is born entirely out of rationality. There are, in this world, things beyond the explanation of man . . . or woman, for that matter,' he added for good measure. 'The desire to understand these things is entirely rational. Now, I think you've had quite enough time. Please, madam, I beg of you, sit down and let us continue with this debate.'

The final say was an invaluable commodity in politics and Sir Tyrrell was pleased to have obtained it. The furious woman sat back down and the discussion returned to more sensible subjects, but there was still an undeniable whiff of change in the air. Sir Tyrrell wondered if this is how it had felt in France prior to the storming of the Bastille. He liked to think England too sensible for such inflammatory nonsense but at times like this he was less sure.

Once the debate was over, he awaited his hansom cab, composing in his head a speech about how the biggest threat facing the world was change, when his thoughts were interrupted.

'Excuse me, Sir Tyrrell, sir,' said a boy.

'You don't have to say "sir" twice,' said the girl next to him.

Both children had a look of the street about them in spite of the newish clothes they wore. The girl held an envelope in her hand.

'What is this?' demanded Sir Tyrrell.

'It's a letter for you, sir,' she replied.

'I have a perfectly functioning letterbox for such things,' replied Sir Tyrrell.

'Sorry sir, we're charged with delivering this letter into your hand,' said the boy. 'Our instructions were clear.'

'Charged by whom?'

Neither child responded so Sir Tyrrell took the envelope. It was indeed addressed to him. He noticed three more identical envelopes in the girl's hand.

'For whom are those destined?' he asked.

'Sorry sir,' she replied. 'We are to give you that letter and say nothing more.'

'I should disregard it entirely for your insolence,' stated Sir Tyrrell, but he couldn't deny he was intrigued. He broke the seal on the envelope and pulled out the letter. On it was written:

For the sole attention of:
Sir Augustus Tyrrell MP
You are invited to join the first meeting of
the Society of Thirteen.
The mysteries of the universe await you.
Your discretion is imperative.

Below was a time, date and the address of a London gentlemen's club located in Piccadilly.

'But who is it from?' Sir Tyrrell's question went unanswered for, when he looked up, the mysterious messengers had vanished.

6

Chains

Tom and Esther were walking along the south side of the Thames on the Albert Embankment, across the river from the Houses of Parliament. The clock tower shone like a beacon, illuminated by a ray of sunshine that had broken through the otherwise grey sky.

'What do you think the letters say?' asked Tom.

'It don't matter,' said Esther. 'Ringmore said he'd likely have more jobs for us after this one.'

'He's a funny one if you ask me,' said Tom. 'Fancy giving us this new clobber just to deliver letters. Could have sent them by post and saved himself the bother.'

'He's paying us, ain't he? Besides, Hardy will lay off if he sees us like this. He'll see we ain't never gonna be his street runners. We're moving up in the world, you and me.' Esther hopped onto a bench, ran along it then jumped off.

'It'll take more than a new pair of trousers to keep Hardy's gang off our backs. Anyway, once Ringmore's done with us, you watch if he don't take these clothes off us and hand us over to the law as punishment for stealing from him.'

'Not after giving us his word,' said Esther.

Rolling black clouds had kept away any romantically inclined couples who might otherwise have been walking hand in hand along the embankment but the threat of a good soaking had not dissuaded the large crowd of people standing on the jetty. Nor had the sporadic rainfall dampened their boisterous spirits.

'Where's this Harry Clay then?' asked Tom.

'Maybe he's arriving by boat,' replied Esther.

The orphans climbed onto a wall to get a better view. A short, stocky man dressed in a white shirt with braces stood at the end of the crowded jetty, tightly bound with thick rope. Tom pointed out a poster on a wall showing the picture of the same man and Esther slowly read the name written above it:

THE REMARKABLE HARRY CLAY

'Do we have any sailors in the crowd?' shouted Clay, who seemed surprisingly calm, considering his predicament.

Several hands shot up.

'I'm afraid I can't point, but you, sir, with the hat. Please step forward.' There was a roughness to Clay's voice, quite unlike the gentrified tones of Lord Ringmore and Sir Tyrrell. 'I would like you to confirm that these ropes are tied as tightly as possible. Anyone else wishing to check can do so after this gentleman. I want you all to know that there is no trickery here. The risk to my life is very real.'

Once the sailor and several other doubting spectators had confirmed the knots were good, Clay asked another volunteer to wrap around several yards of chain that lay at his feet. The final touch came in the form of a bag tied securely over his head, hiding his face and muffling his voice.

'And now I, the remarkable Harry Clay, will plunge into the cold waters of the River Thames, subjecting myself to the strong currents that will try to drag me down while I attempt to free myself from these layers of bondage. Due to many years of training I am able to hold my breath for two and a half minutes. That is how long I have to escape. Two and a half minutes. Those of you with pocket watches, I ask that you keep time. If after two and a half minutes I have not surfaced, then you may fear the worst and you can tell everyone that you witnessed the death of Harry Clay.' He paused for dramatic effect. 'Hopefully not though, eh?'

The crowd laughed uneasily. They had turned up to be astounded, not to witness an overly complicated suicide.

'Begin timing . . . NOW.' Clay leapt backwards and landed with a tremendous splash in the water.

'Oh well,' said Tom. 'One less letter to deliver. He'll never get out of all that.'

'Wait,' said Esther.

Everyone watched the surface of the water anxiously. The crowd gasped when bubbles surfaced and a voice cried, 'One minute.'

'He'll never do it,' said another.

'It's impossible,' said a third.

Esther felt as though she could taste the crowd's fear and excitement.

'Two minutes,' yelled an eager timekeeper.

'Look!' shouted a woman.

The bag that had been around Clay's head surfaced and floated away, carried by the current.

'He must have drowned,' cried a panicked voice.

'Or been poisoned, jumping into that filthy old river,' said another.

'Someone do something,' yelled a woman.

'Two and half minutes.'

'He's a gonner,' said Tom.

'No, look,' said Esther.

This time it was the rope that appeared.

'Three minutes,' yelled a voice.

'Over there, Tom,' said Esther. With every eye watching the spot where he had gone under, no one in the crowd noticed a dripping figure climb up a set of steps on the other side of the jetty. Moving with the easy agility of a monkey, Clay clambered up onto a large metal pillar which supported the jetty. At the top he adopted a victorious pose, with his legs together and his arms in the air.

A drop of water fell from one of his soaking sleeves and alerted the crowd to his presence. A lady screamed and the entire crowd swung round to see the man standing on top of the huge pillar. The awed silence was broken by sudden, overjoyed applause and cries of 'Miracle!', 'Incredible!' and 'Remarkable!'

A well-dressed man stepped out in front of the crowd and addressed them. 'If you enjoyed that you can come and be amazed again when the remarkable Mr Clay takes to the stage of my Theatre Royal, Victoria, next week.'

With this man diverting the crowd's attention, Clay made his way quickly up the gangway. He speedily towelled himself dry, then slipped into a fresh shirt. By the time he was level with Tom and Esther he had pulled a hat over his head and become virtually invisible to the crowd that had been enraptured by his stunt. To Esther, who had some experience in vanishing into crowds herself, this was as remarkable a feat as the escape from the water.

She jumped off the wall and landed in front of him. 'Mr Clay,' she said.

A second man appeared and pushed her to the side.

'Oi, watch who you're pushing,' said Tom.

'Harry Clay doesn't give autographs,' said the man, who looked about the same age as Clay but wore a crooked top hat on his head and a thick moustache on his upper lip.

'It's all right, Fred,' said Clay, spying the envelope in Esther's hand. 'Providing you have a pen, I'll make an exception this once.'

'It's not for signing,' said Esther. 'It's a letter for you.'

'How kind,' Clay replied. He took it from her. She watched his eyebrows rise as he read its contents. Whatever these letters said, they were obviously enough to intrigue a man as intriguing as the Remarkable Harry Clay.

7

Language

The third envelope took the orphans to Bedford Square. The houses here had several steps leading up to the front door, as though they were far too grand to stand at street level. Iron gates in front of the steps provided an extra layer of protection from the outside world. It was the kind of area that afforded good opportunities for the quick witted and the light fingered, but Tom and Esther had never before had cause to knock on one of the doors.

It was opened by a tall man with skin the colour and texture of tree bark. His clothes were made not from cotton or wool but from exotic animal hides. Tom nudged Esther and pointed at his bare feet.

'We have a letter for Mr Symmonds,' said Esther.

The man held out a huge hand to take the letter but Esther kept it back. 'It is to be delivered into Mr Symmonds' hand only,' she said.

The man stared silently.

'How do you know this ain't Symmonds?' said Tom to Esther, keen to get away.

'He don't look like a John Symmonds to me,' replied Esther.

The man turned and walked into one of the rooms, leaving the door open. They heard voices from within, speaking a language they could not understand. After a brief exchange, a second man appeared at the doorway. He was smaller and paler than the first, dressed in a fussy suit and with thick sideburns framing his flushed cheeks.

'Yes? Can I help you?' he asked.

'You John Symmonds?' asked Tom.

'Oh, very interesting. Don't say another word.' The man looked at the orphans with great curiosity and rubbed his chin. 'No. I'll need more. Please repeat after me: *Where are the hares? They should have waited. Those tattered old creatures. Where have they gone? They are running away.*'

Tom and Esther looked at each other.

'Please, if you would be so kind,' said the man, insistently.

'*Where are the 'ares?*' said Tom. '*They should've waited. Those tattered old creatures. Where've they gone? They're runnin' away.* What flippin' 'ares you on about?'

'Excellent. So what do we have? Two smartly dressed minors, apparently employed in some kind of postal capacity and yet from the dropped Hs and Gs; the habitual glottal stops; the insistent contractions and the flattened vowels, I'd place you amongst the sub-criminal classes of London. Though I do detect some education, which would suggest that you have spent time either in a ragged school or an orphanage. There is a hint of an Irish inflection in your speech, so I'll guess a Catholic orphanage. How did I do?'

'How did you know all that?' asked Tom.

'To a linguist such as myself the human voice is as revealing as a man's attire. Take my man, Kiyaya. You did not need to hear him speak to know that he travelled a great distance to be here, did you? You could tell by his appearance.'

The huge man stood silently behind him.

'Where's he from then?' asked Esther.

'He is a native of America. A fascinating country, linguistically speaking. Kiyaya here speaks only his native tongue.'

'He don't say much,' said Tom.

'In his own language he is capable of great loquacity. He is here helping me with my book. I am writing a detailed account of the many languages and dialects of America. Fascinating subject. He also acts as my manservant. Between you and I though, he makes terrible tea.' Mr Symmonds chuckled.

Kiyaya's face remained as impassive as before, showing no recognition that he was the subject of the conversation.

'Now, what is it you are delivering?' asked Mr Symmonds.

Esther handed him the letter and watched him open and read it. 'What a mysterious missive,' he said. 'How many of these are you delivering?'

'We've got one more to go,' said Tom.

8

Novelist

The fourth envelope was addressed to a Mr G. Hayman, but when the orphans called on the door of his Soho town house, they were informed by the housekeeper that Mr Hayman was currently residing in Brighton. Since Lord Ringmore had issued strict instructions that the letter be delivered by the following evening, Esther asked for an address where he could be located. The housekeeper, a young woman with sharp blue eyes, replied that Mr G. Hayman did not want to be disturbed in Brighton, but the orphans were quite adamant and eventually she relented and furnished them with the address, requesting that they did not reveal it came from her.

Lord Ringmore had provided the orphans with money for train fares but as they had spent it on breakfast Tom suggested they sneak on board a train at London Bridge. They spent the journey hiding from the ticket inspector and, when the train pulled into Brighton, jumped off and easily outran the station guard. Outside the station, Esther asked a grocer for directions to the address while Tom stole a couple of pears to eat on the way.

'Have you noticed how much easier swiping is dressed up all respectable like?' said Tom, as they walked up a steep hill.

'Yeah, if you look like you've got money why would you steal?' said Esther.

'I'd still steal even if I had all the money in the world,' said Tom. He took a large bite from his pear. 'Swiped stuff tastes better than bought stuff.'

When they reached the address at the top of the hill, they pressed the bell for the upper-floor flat and waited until an upstairs window slid open.

'Go away,' called a low voice.

'We've a delivery for Mr G. Hayman,' said Esther.

'Mr G. Hayman, the world renowned novelist hailed by the *New York Times* as one of the most important writers of a generation?' said the voice. There was something odd about its tone. There was an American accent, but it wasn't just that.

'We have a letter for him,' said Esther. 'We're to deliver it into his hand alone.'

'Well, I'm afraid his hands are currently otherwise engaged in the act of writing his latest bestseller,' replied the odd voice.

'People only write with one hand,' said Esther. 'Perhaps he could use the other to take this letter then we can be on our way.'

'Oh, for goodness' sake, wait there.'

The window slammed shut again and the orphans heard footsteps coming down the stairs. They saw a movement behind the frosted glass. They were expecting the silhouette to belong to Mr Hayman himself so it was a surprise when the door opened and they found themselves staring at an attractive young woman with neatly cropped hair and a smart, tailored gentleman's suit.

'For all the deadly perils faced by my hero, I fear he will eventually fall foul of death by interruption,' snapped the woman. 'Come on then, let's have this letter.'

'I'm sorry, lady,' said Tom. 'We've instructions to deliver it directly to Mr Hayman.'

The woman held out her hand. 'I assure you that this is the hand you seek,' she said. 'And if you continue to waste its time it will soon be clipping you around the ear.'

'You ain't a fella,' said Tom. 'You're a lady.'

The woman gasped with mock horror. 'A lady?' she said. 'You think a delicate lady's hand could have penned such richly woven classics as *The Contract of Alderly Edge*, *The Malmesbury Mystery* and *The Bloodstain of Boulge Hall*?'

'I . . .' began Tom.

'Tom,' said Esther. 'I think this is Mr G. Hayman.'

'At least one of you has a brain,' said the woman. 'No surprises that it is the female.'

Tom sulkily handed over the letter.

The author opened it, quickly skimmed its contents and looked at the orphans. 'I'll wager that Lord Ringmore is behind all this,' she said. 'I swear he contrives to have more mystery and drama in his life than I could ever cram into one of my novels. Now, I'll have to ask you both to leave. If I am to make this appointment I will have to double my efforts to get this novel finished.'

She winked at Esther then slammed the door in their faces.

9

Formation

When Miss Georgina Waters had first arrived in London ten years ago from New York she had been struck by the differences. If England was the motherland, she wondered, then why was it so relentlessly male in its attitudes? It had been her publisher's idea to use a male pseudonym for her first novel. She had spoken out vehemently against it at first but, since her fiction relied so heavily on elements of the supernatural, she saw the point that under female authorship, the critics could too easily dismiss her book as irrelevant fancy. Her publisher's instincts had proved sound. *The Contract of Alderly Edge* had been well reviewed, widely read and hugely profitable. With more successes she retained the name but it became less important to hide her true identity.

Over time, Georgina Waters had grown into the role of Mr G. Hayman. Sometimes she considered the author to be her greatest creation of all. Neither wholly man nor fully a woman, Mr G. Hayman was something different. Something new.

She was well accustomed to reactions such as that of the doorman at the club, who took her coat. His slow registering of the undeniable femininity of her shoulders, the embarrassed lowering of his gaze, subtly taking in the curve of the waist, emphasised rather than hidden by the bespoke suit, his inevitable furtive glance at her chest. Mr G. Hayman enjoyed the confusion she caused.

She did not wear such clothes as a disguise. She wore no false whiskers on her face. She dressed and acted precisely as she chose. She swanned into this exclusively gentlemen's club without apology. Her confidence gave her power over the poor confused males who struggled to reconcile her behaviour with the obvious evidence of her sex. As usual, the doorman's inner turmoil was all too obvious. Should he say something? He knew the rules dictated *No ladies*, but Mr G. Hayman's confidence caused him to doubt his own eyes.

'Will sir be dining or drinking this evening?' asked the doorman, finally shutting out the part of his brain that told him this was a woman.

Mr G. Hayman showed him the invitation.

'Very good, sir,' said the doorman. 'You are expected in the study on the third floor. Someone will be up presently to take your drinks order.'

Mr G. Hayman nodded in thanks and made her way up the stairs, aware that the doorman would not be able to resist watching and that the sight of her posterior would be causing him yet more inner turmoil.

As with most of London's clubs, Mr G. Hayman found this one depressingly dark. The panelling was always made from the darkest wood. The lamps provided a gloomy atmosphere and the furniture was abysmally faded and worn. She used to believe London's clubs were like this for fear of waking their nearly dead members, but over time she had developed a new theory. These clubs provided sanctuaries where the wealthy and powerful could hide from the ever-changing world which daily encroached on their existence.

Outside the study on the third floor there stood a man as tall as the door frame itself. From his colouring and dress she took him to be a native of her own country. He took one look at the invitation in her hand and stood to the side.

Of the three men inside the study, she recognised only one.

'Harry Clay,' she said. 'Why, I should have guessed you'd be involved in this business.'

'Mr G. Hayman,' replied Clay.

'Mister . . . ?' said the older, larger of the other two gentlemen, who looked quite at home in this fusty old club.

'Sir Tyrrell, Mr Symmonds, this is Mr G. Hayman, the critically acclaimed novelist who plunders the superstitions of our land and turns them into extremely profitable fiction.'

'I am aware of your work. I had no idea you were . . .' Mr Symmonds faltered.

'So young. Yes, I am often told as much,' said Mr G. Hayman.

'John here also writes,' said Clay, continuing his adopted role of master of ceremonies.

'My output is nowhere as imaginative as yours. My published books tackle the subject of linguistics,' said Mr Symmonds.

'How many languages do you speak now, John?' asked Clay.

'Ah well, one has to distinguish between a language and a dialect.'

'Never one for a straight answer, is John,' said Mr Clay. 'And this is Sir Tyrrell, high-ranking Member of Parliament and unashamed explorer of the occult.'

'Pleased to meet you,' said Sir Tyrrell, who appeared to have recovered from his initial shock. 'I actually read one of your novels. I found it most diverting.'

'Thank you,' said Mr G. Hayman.

'So here we all are,' said Clay. 'A politician, a linguist, a novelist and an illusionist. It feels as if we are still lacking, wouldn't you say? My invitation referred to this as the Society of Thirteen.'

'The title does not refer to our number.' Lord Ringmore stepped into the room, walking stick in hand.

'Ah, our mystery summoner,' said Mr G. Hayman.

'I am glad I was able to intrigue you all sufficiently to turn up at such short notice.' Lord Ringmore turned the key to lock the door behind him. 'I know you are all busy people and I hope you know enough of me to understand that I would not waste your time.'

'You and I have often disagreed on what constitutes a

waste of time,' said Clay.

'Indeed we have, Harry,' replied Lord Ringmore. 'But tonight I am confident that I will reveal to you something truly astonishing.'

'Going by the presence of Mr Hayman and Sir Tyrrell I presume we are talking matters of the occult, and you know where I stand on that subject,' said Clay.

'I believe that even Harry Clay, the great sceptic, will be impressed,' said Lord Ringmore.

'In my experience there's nothing more remarkable in the world than man's ability to believe remarkable things,' replied Clay.

'A fact which you have exploited to great effect,' muttered Sir Tyrrell.

'Mr Clay's dogged cynicism will help verify the validity of my discovery,' said Lord Ringmore. 'But before we go any further I must ask that you all give me your solemn vow that nothing you learn here will ever be mentioned outside of this circle.'

'You have my word,' said Sir Tyrrell.

'And mine,' said Mr Symmonds.

'Discretion is my middle name,' said Mr G. Hayman.

'How can I promise not to speak of something I haven't seen yet?' asked Clay.

'In which case, I offer you this caveat, Harry,' said Lord Ringmore. 'You will not speak of anything you see this evening until you can satisfactorily explain it yourself.'

'You mean while it remains a mystery it remains a secret,' summarised Clay. 'Now, there's a deal I will happily accept.'

'Good. You have been a great teacher to me in penetrating the trickery used by those who claim great powers for the sake of profit,' said Lord Ringmore.

'What about me?' asked Mr Symmonds. 'I have never expressed an opinion in spiritualism, one way or the other.'

'No. Language is your passion, John,' replied Lord Ringmore. 'And I'm hoping your linguistic skills will prove invaluable.'

'So we all have parts to play in this game of yours?' asked Sir Tyrrell.

'Each Society member will be expected to contribute,' said Lord Ringmore. 'You, Sir Tyrrell, have accompanied me on many of my exploratory journeys, whereas no one is better read in the matters of all things supernatural than Mr G. Hayman.'

'And what do you bring, Ringmore?' asked Mr G. Hayman. 'Other than the obvious flair for mystery and melodrama?'

'A discovery.' Lord Ringmore pulled out from his cloak a book, which he threw onto a table between them.

'You've discovered a book. Well done you,' said Clay, offering a slow hand-clap.

Mr Symmonds picked it up. He examined the shape on the back and the number on the front. 'I'm guessing these numerals are the reason for the Society's name?' he said.

'Thirteen,' said Mr G. Hayman, thoughtfully.

'I have gathered you to help me decipher this book and its meaning,' said Lord Ringmore.

Mr Symmonds leafed through the pages. 'This is no

language. It is a collection of shapes.'

'Is the written word not formed of shapes?' asked Lord Ringmore.

'Yes, but if this is a language I see no influence of Latin, Celtic nor any Scandinavian languages. I would have to consult my books on Arabic and African script but . . .'

'Perhaps I would be better suited to deciphering it,' said Sir Tyrrell. 'After all, I have dedicated a great many hours to the study of magical languages, reading runes and suchlike.'

'Magical languages.' Mr Symmonds snorted.

Clay laughed. 'Yes. Why on earth are we to believe that this is anything but a child's scribbling pad? No, don't tell me. It was sold to you by a Welsh druid who held a staff and spoke in tongues?'

Lord Ringmore smiled patiently. 'Please, Mr Symmonds,' he said. 'Would you be so kind as to hand the book around. Let everyone have a look.'

John Symmonds did as he was asked and the book was passed from hand to hand until it reached Clay.

'Any thoughts?' asked Lord Ringmore.

'It certainly has age,' said Mr G. Hayman. 'Also, the number thirteen reminds me of something I have come across in my research.'

'Yes. It is unlucky for some,' said Sir Tyrrell.

'Many of our superstitions have their roots in magical lore,' said Mr G. Hayman. 'I will consult my notes regarding this book, but I'm afraid at present I am edging towards Clay's cynicism.'

'Then let us return to basics,' said Lord Ringmore. 'From what material would you say it was made?'

'Aren't all books made from paper?' asked Sir Tyrrell. 'Now really, what is the point of all this, Ringmore?'

'Paper rips, does it not?' replied Lord Ringmore. 'Mr Clay, perhaps you would care to tear a page out of the book?'

'With pleasure,' replied Clay. He took a page in his hand and tugged, but the book remained intact. He tried to tear a page. He tried another but none would come free from the book. Nor could he make even the smallest rip on the paper. 'A very neat trick,' he admitted. 'I'm guessing some kind of rubberised solution has been added to the book. I could definitely use a prop like this in my show.'

'You are probably right that this is a counterfeit sold to me by a trickster,' said Lord Ringmore. 'In fact, why don't you do us all a favour and toss the book into the fire?'

The others stared at Lord Ringmore.

'Into the fire?' said Clay.

'Into the fire,' stated Lord Ringmore.

'Very well.'

Clay threw the book into the fireplace. The yellow flames shot up as it landed on the smouldering wood.

'What a curious evening's entertainment this is,' said Mr Symmonds.

'Your curiosity is the least of my goals.' Lord Ringmore picked up a pair of tongs, lifted the book from the flames and dropped it back onto the table. To the astonishment of everyone in the room, the book looked exactly as it had before it was thrown into the fire. The paper was not blackened or burnt, and there was not even a blemish on it, nor anything to suggest that it had just been at the centre of a roaring fire. Mr G. Hayman picked up the book again.

'It's not even warm,' she said.

Lord Ringmore smiled. 'The Society of Thirteen has been formed to investigate this remarkable object. I believe that such an inquiry will reveal the truth about magic. With the combined investigative minds and the resources at our disposal, I think we can penetrate the secrets of this book.'

'The book has my interest and you have my silence,' said Mr Clay.

'Excellent,' said Lord Ringmore. 'It is vital that no word is spoken of this outside our circle. Mr Symmonds' man may accompany him as there is no danger of his overhearing, but I ask that you only speak of these matters when in a safe and secure environment. Trust no one. Magic disappeared from our land many centuries ago. If we are to reawaken its power, we must do so with great caution. Now, I suggest that we go downstairs and eat. I have a private dining room reserved and we must discuss the way to progress. I should like Mr Symmonds to take the book first so that he may attempt to discover its meaning.' Lord Ringmore slipped the book back into his cloak and led the others out of the room.

With the study empty, the only movement in the room was the gentle flickering of the fire, until the doors of a cabinet burst open and Tom and Esther crawled out from their hiding place.

10

Hardy

Sometimes Tom didn't understand Esther at all. After making so much fuss about not betraying Lord Ringmore's trust, it had been her idea to sneak inside the club, and hide inside the cabinet. It wasn't the first time she had said one thing then done the opposite, either. It just went to show that no one was completely trustworthy.

Back in Rotherhithe, the orphans discussed what they had overheard.

'If you ask me, the whole thing is a swindle,' said Tom.

'Who's swindling who?' asked Esther.

'I reckon it's Lord Ringmore tricking the rest of them,' he replied. 'You heard him. Everyone has to contribute. You watch if he don't start asking for money. He's going to use this book to get serious coin out of the others.'

'I never heard of a Lord short of a bob or two,' said Esther, doubtfully.

'Don't you believe it,' said Tom. 'I'll bet half these Lords and Barons and what have you don't have no real money. They live in big houses but they can't afford the coal for the fire. Now I think on it, I didn't see no servants at his place. Maybe he ain't even a real Lord. We were saying ourselves how much easier it is to trick folk if you look like you don't need money.'

'I wouldn't want to try and get any scheme past that Harry Clay,' said Esther. 'Hayman didn't seem like no dummy, neither.'

'Maybe they're in on it too. Maybe the whole thing is about getting money off the fat politician. He looks like he's got proper coinage.'

Esther laughed. 'You've got too much imagination.'

'You have to admit that this has everything you need for a good swindle. A fanciful story, a convincing prop . . .'

'But what if it ain't?' said Esther. 'You heard what they said about it being impossible to destroy.'

'We couldn't see a thing in there. It was probably a trick, with two different books.'

'But what if the book really is magic? Imagine.'

Tom snorted. 'The only magic I care about is the magic of money.'

The next day, when the orphans turned up on Lord Ringmore's doorstep, he handed them payment and told them that their next task was to keep watch outside Mr Symmonds' house, explaining that 'Mr Symmonds has in his possession a book of great value to me. I want you to ensure that neither he nor it leave the house. If he does leave, one of you will follow him, the other will inform me.'

An hour later the orphans were hidden behind a bush in the communal garden at the centre of Bedford Square. It was a cold day to be standing outside and Tom was feeling restless so was pleased when Mr Symmonds' door opened and his manservant stepped out. 'Come on, let's follow him,' urged Tom.

'Ringmore only told us to watch Symmonds,' said Esther.

The American Indian closed the door behind him. Over his broad shoulders he wore a heavily furred animal skin to protect him from the cold. In his hand he carried a long stick, the tip of which was carved into the head of an eagle.

'Yeah, but we don't know this fella ain't got the book,' said Tom. 'I should follow him. I'll watch where he goes. You stay here and watch the house.'

'All right, but don't get seen.'

Tom took after him, feeling much happier to be on the move. Kiyaya walked with huge strides, meaning Tom had to run to keep up. He kept his distance as the Indian headed towards the bustling streets of Holborn. He was easy enough to follow. If Tom did lose sight of him for a moment, he simply had to look for the trail of turning heads the enormous man left in his wake. Tom had no idea what this man's homeland was like but he reckoned it was likely to be pretty different from Holborn. Yet the Indian didn't seem at all concerned by the chaos of the city. He crossed the busy road with the confidence of a native Londoner. It was Tom who got shouted at by a hansom cab driver as he darted after him. Tom shrugged off the driver's insults and found a lamp post from which to watch as the Indian entered a butcher's shop.

'Hello, Tom. Where's your girlfriend?'

Tom didn't need to turn around to know who had spoken. He felt a hand on his shoulder. The grip tightened and forced him to turn. Hardy stood behind him with his hands in his pockets. He wore the same grubby coat as always and kept the same company. Brewer, Worms and Stump were all former pupils of St Clement's Catholic School for Waifs and Strays. Hardy was the oldest, but it was Stump who held Tom and kept him from legging it. The gangly limbed Worms was next to him, while Brewer, the youngest of the gang, allowed Tom a brief glimpse of his blade, showing him what would happen if he tried to run off.

'What do you want, Hardy?' said Tom. 'I'm busy.'

'Busy, is it? Busy doing what? Busy working my patch? Busy taking money from the people in my protection? Busy stealing from me, Tom? That kind of busy, Tom, is it?'

'No.'

'Busy coming up with excuses why you shouldn't pay me what you owe me?'

'We don't owe nothing,' said Tom.

'Everyone owes,' said Hardy. 'And everyone pays, sooner or later. Tell me what you're doing on this fine morning if you ain't picking no pockets. You out doing a spot of shopping, are you?'

'It ain't your business,' said Tom.

'Anything that happens on my patch is my business and you know full well this is my patch.'

'Me and Esther have got a job.'

'What job?'

'We're running errands for some gent.'

'Which would explain this fancy clobber you're wearing. What kind of errands?'

'What's it matter?' replied Tom.

Stump bent Tom's arm behind his back. The pain was unbearable but Tom remained silent.

'I always liked you, Tom,' said Hardy. 'I remember your first day. What were you? Five years old? You were crying because your auntie had left you. You told everyone that she was going to come back for you. Never did though, did she? Remember, boys?'

The others laughed cruelly.

Tom stared back angrily.

'What you really up to, Tom?' asked Hardy.

'This fella caught us thievin' from him,' said Tom. 'It weren't round here. It was over Piccadilly way. But instead of shopping us he's got us delivering messages and that. It's nothing. Just a few coins is all.'

'Sounds peculiar if you ask me. I tell you what, you give me my cut and you'll be on your way. No trouble.'

'I told you, it wasn't on your patch.'

'And yet here you are, on my patch now.' Hardy spoke quietly in Tom's ear. 'You know that sooner or later you'll end up working for me, but think about it. If it's you that comes to me, rather than Esther, I'll look on you more favourably, won't I? She makes all the decisions for you. I know that. But you got a brain just the same as her. You can make your own choices.'

'I already make my own choices.'

'Glad to hear it. Just make sure they're the wise ones, eh?'

'I don't take orders from you.'

'No, that's what Esther's for.' Hardy laughed. 'And don't go thinking you're safe in that Rotherhithe warehouse neither.'

Tom said nothing and tried to keep his expression blank.

'Didn't think I knew that one, did you? But you got no secrets from me. Or, at least, you'd be wise not to have. Now, Stump is going to leave you with a little reminder that I'm not messing about.'

Stump yanked Tom's arm further behind his back. Tom could feel the bone creak. Much further and it would break altogether. 'Please don't,' he begged.

'It's too late for pleading,' said Stump.

Tom closed his eyes and awaited the inevitable snap but just as the pain reached an unbearable level, suddenly it was gone. With his arm free, Tom turned to see Kiyaya holding Stump in the air, his short legs dangling.

'Put him down,' said Hardy, his voice bubbling with barely controlled fury.

'What's going on?' asked Stump, unable to see who was holding him.

'Put him down, you savage,' hissed Hardy.

Brewer began to take his knife out but Hardy stopped him with a wave of his hand. All around, people were stopping to stare at the extraordinary sight of the enormous man holding the boy in the air. Apparently not so keen on the attention, Kiyaya placed Stump back on the ground.

'Nothing to see here,' shouted Hardy aggressively at the gawking onlookers, staring each one of them down until they walked away and went back to minding their own business. He turned to Tom. 'Interesting company you're keeping these days, Tom,' he said, and he and his gang vanished into the crowd, leaving Tom alone with the Indian.

The huge man looked at Tom, his intense dark eyes boring into him.

'Why d'you do that?' asked Tom.

In response, Kiyaya reached out a hand. Tom stepped back, avoiding contact. Something about Kiyaya's dark eyes filled Tom with dread. He turned and fled.

II

Magpie

London had its fair share of bedraggled birds with missing legs, tattered feathers and damaged wings, but Esther had never seen a magpie in such a state as the one which hopped across Bedford Square towards her.

'Morning Mister Magpie,' she said. She had been taught to greet magpies like this by Sister Eucharia, a superstitious nun who had once told the class that, being the devil's bird, a magpie could receive the gift of speech by a drop of human blood on its tongue. When Mother Agnes, the prioress, got wind of this she had hauled Sister Eucharia out in front of the entire school and admonished her for teaching such irreligious nonsense, but the lesson had stuck with Esther and it came back as she watched the mangy magpie boldly hopping towards her, squawking loudly. As it got closer, Esther saw what a sorry state it was in. Its feathers were worn. It walked with a distinct limp and one of its eyes hung out of its socket.

'Shoo,' she said, disgusted by the bird. 'Go away.'

The magpie didn't flinch.

Esther jumped forward and clapped her hands. The magpie remained unperturbed by her efforts to frighten it. Esther had never seen a bird act in such a way. Something rubbed against her leg. She looked down and saw a black cat arching its back and pushing itself against her shin.

'Hello there,' she said, scratching its back.

The cat kept its green eyes focused on the bird.

The magpie looked as though it would stand its ground until the cat prowled forward with a threatening, low purr. Deciding the cat meant business, the magpie spread its wings and flew to the safety of a nearby rooftop. Esther bent down to pick the cat up, but at that moment Tom returned and his arrival startled the cat and sent it running into the undergrowth.

'Where's the Indian?' she asked.

'There.' Tom pointed to where Kiyaya was coming around the corner.

'What happened?' asked Esther. 'How did you get ahead of him?'

'Just did,' mumbled Tom. 'He went to the butcher's, is all.'

Esther had known Tom since the age of five. They had grown up together. She knew when he was hiding something. 'He saw you, didn't he?'

'Not a chance. It was just dull is all. This whole business is dull if you ask me. The sooner we get back to what we do best, the better.'

Esther knew he wasn't telling her everything but she also knew that there was no point pushing him.

By five o'clock, it was dark except for the yellow light spilling down from the streetlamps, but even in the gloom there was no question as to the identity of Mr Symmonds' visitor. His face may have been hidden beneath his top hat but Lord Ringmore was identifiable by his purposeful stride and by the tap-tap-tapping of his walking stick along the pavement. Before knocking on the door he turned to peer into the darkness in search of Tom and Esther. When the door opened he went inside, re-emerging half an hour later and immediately crossing the road towards the orphans. In his hand he held the book. The number thirteen was visible on the cover.

'Got your book back then,' said Tom.

Lord Ringmore tucked it out of sight. 'Yes. Now I have another task for you,' he said plainly.

The orphans stepped out from behind the bush.

'We haven't been paid for this one,' said Tom.

Lord Ringmore reached into his pocket and pulled out a couple of coins but held them out of reach. 'The day is not yet done,' he said. 'First you are to gather the other three and tell them to meet at nine o'clock at the same place as last night.'

'Nine o'clock this evening?' said Esther. 'There's no time to reach them all before then.'

'There is if we split up,' said Tom.

'Split up?' said Esther, surprised to hear Tom making

useful suggestions when he didn't even want to do the job.

'Yeah, you could tell Clay and Sir Tyrrell, while I go to Soho and tell Hayman,' he said.

'I do not care how you achieve it, but you won't get paid until this task is completed,' replied Lord Ringmore. 'As before, ensure that you speak directly to each individual. Involve no one else. No servants, no housekeepers, no butlers.'

'You don't trust servants, do you?' asked Tom. 'I mean, I noticed you ain't got none yourself.'

'I would sooner employ thieves and pickpockets than the serving classes. At least they are more honest about their occupations,' said Lord Ringmore.

'That why you got us working for you?' asked Tom.

'I suggest you do not give me reason to change my mind about that,' said Lord Ringmore, raising his stick threateningly.

'There's no need for that,' said Tom.

'We'd better get moving if we're to reach everyone in time,' said Esther, tugging Tom's sleeve.

'I would spend more time listening to the girl if I were you,' said Lord Ringmore. 'I have not employed you to answer me back. If you are to continue earning, it would do you good to remember that.'

12

Mondriat

Mondriat landed on the rooftop and peered over the edge. The black cat had gone again. What was it about that cat? he wondered. A gust of icy cold wind sent a cloud of black smoke from a nearby chimney in his direction, making him shiver and cough. He hopped along the roof to escape the smoke.

Coughing was a funny thing. He had never seen any other birds do it, but every revolting feathered body Mondriat had inhabited over the years had been the same. They shivered and coughed and choked. They even sneezed. He felt the bitterness of life in a way animals did not. Such was the curse of the familiar, he thought, to experience all the pain of humanity without any of the benefits.

Looking down at the square, he saw the orphan girl retreat to her hiding place. He wondered what he had been thinking, trying to speak to her like that. He hadn't really expected her to understand him, but was still disappointed when she had turned to look at him and said the three words he detested most in the world.

'Morning Mister Magpie.'

Given the tirade of abuse that he'd hurled at her, it was probably a good thing that the girl had not been able to understand. But still, the orphans interested him greatly. Why were they watching the book too? This whole business was intriguing. And how wonderful to be intrigued, after all this time.

Since being confined to these decaying animal bodies, the world had been an interminably dull, flat place. Mondriat chose birds' bodies because he liked being able to fly but, as time dragged on, he had often contemplated flying into the side of a building and ending it all. It was only his high self-regard and strong aversion to pain that prevented him from going through with it. Instead, he clung onto this pitiful existence in the hope that one day he might experience the splendour and magnificence of Conjury again. Having played his own part in its demise he lived to see it return.

The book offered this opportunity. After far too long spent living on worms and squabbling with pigeons over scraps, finally it would all be worthwhile.

The book had first come to Mondriat's attention a few weeks ago when he had felt something different in London's stale air. He had stretched his wings and taken to the sky, where he saw a glow more wonderful than any sunset. More colourful than a rainbow. More hopeful than the song of a lark. London's drab inhabitants were utterly oblivious to its splendour but, to Mondriat, it was unmistakable and utterly breathtaking. At long last his tired eyes were witnessing the ripples of pure Conjury.

He had immediately begun to search out the cause of this shift. Could a Conjuror have arrived from a distant land? Or perhaps someone had performed the Creation Spell by accident? Flying over the city he had discovered that the disturbances had come from the smouldering remains of a burnt-out shop, south of the river. Mondriat had watched from a nearby roof, tail twitching excitedly until he saw the unfortunate shop owner enter the building, loudly bemoaning his misfortune and searching for any items that had survived the incineration. When this man had emerged clutching a book, Mondriat knew he had found the source. The book's protective spell must have lain dormant all these years but, when endangered by the fire, the Conjury had awoken to protect it.

The black cat had been prowling around there then, too. Could it really be a coincidence? How did all this fit together? The book. The orphans. The Lord. The cat. Whatever was going on, Mondriat was determined to learn the truth and, if at all possible, turn it to his own advantage.

13

Thirteen

Lord Ringmore sat in the upstairs study of the club, watching the flickering fire. As the clock chimed the ninth hour, he pulled out his pocket watch to confirm its accuracy and considered his wisdom in leaving so much in the hands of a pair of ragged street orphans. Thankfully, his faith was restored when all four remaining Society members entered the room within five minutes of each other.

'We meet again so soon?' said Clay. 'Could it be that the great John Symmonds has penetrated the secrets of this book already?'

'I have made some good copies but I'm afraid I am still at very early stages,' said Mr Symmonds. 'At this point I am still ruling things out. Having dismissed Latin, Greek, German and Celtic, I have been scouring what I can find on Asian, African and Arabic for some kind of connection, but with no joy as of yet. I am still doubtful that we are dealing with a language at all. Even the pictorial texts, such as ancient Egypt's hieroglyphics, involve more systematic repetition than is found in this book.'

'Perhaps it would be better to leave the decoding to those of us who have greater experience in the area,' said Sir Tyrrell.

'Oh, yes,' said Clay. 'Sir Tyrrell is fluent in the ancient language of Hoaxus Pocus.'

'And what qualifications have you, other than the ability to repeatedly escape from tampered locks?' said Sir Tyrrell.

'Tampered?' exclaimed Clay. 'I've sued men for saying so.'

'Gentlemen, please,' said Lord Ringmore. 'This bickering will achieve nothing. Everyone will get a chance to examine the book. In the meantime, I have called this meeting because Mr Hayman has new information.'

'Thank you, Lord Ringmore.' Mr G. Hayman stood up and bid the others sit. 'Society members, I have spent many years delving into the true history of your little island as research for my novel writing.'

Sir Tyrrell snorted derisively. 'Forgive me, but I hardly think your novels the first port of call when one seeks an accurate account of our rich history. As I recall from the one I read, you misplaced several of our key battles both in time and place.'

'Well, yes,' said Mr G. Hayman. 'I'm sure when you think of history you think of that which has been written down in books, but the history of England is more than a list of squabbling kings and queens. It is more than an account of every battle won and lost. I have precious little interest in these petty skirmishes.'

'So I have noticed,' said Sir Tyrrell.

'What interests me is the undocumented history,' continued Mr G. Hayman. 'The history that is passed down in memory and folklore. I have travelled the length and breadth of the British Isles and everywhere I go, I search for those who remember, but whose voices are rarely heard.' She pulled out of her bag a pile of bound notepads.

'Which voices are those then?' demanded Sir Tyrrell.

'Mostly, female voices.' Mr G. Hayman opened one of the books to a page filled with reams of neatly written notes, diagrams and pictures. 'In every village and town I visit I interview the elders about the things which they remember and the things they have heard. The real stories of this land are not of the battlefields but of the dark, secluded corners where strange things occur, the places where superstitions lurk and folklore thrives. This is where one may discover the truth about the practitioners of magic who were once commonplace in this land, known amongst themselves as the Infected.'

'*Infected*?' repeated Sir Tyrrell. 'Infected with what?'

'It's said they were infected with a substance they call the lifeblood, a source of power that flows directly from the Earthsoul.'

'I hadn't realised we were here to listen to fairy stories,' said Clay.

'The natural inclination to doubt these things has always been encouraged by those who know the truth. The power the Infected wielded was phenomenal, but it was nothing without secrecy. In your version of history the Infected are shadows, hidden behind the puppet figures they manipulated.'

'And what have these notes of yours to tell us about our durable little book?' asked Sir Tyrrell.

'When I first saw this book it brought to mind an object I had once been told about, but I had to check my research to be sure.' Mr G. Hayman flicked to a page where she had written the number thirteen and drawn a box around it. 'It is known as *The Book of Thirteen* and it was written by Olwyn Broe.'

'Should we know the name?' asked Clay.

'She was a Conjuress,' replied Mr G. Hayman. 'What you might call a witch.'

'Do we know what this book was used for?' asked Lord Ringmore.

'I'm still looking into that, but the stories of *The Book of Thirteen* match the book in our possession. You see, it is named after the numbers which adorn its cover . . . the number thirteen.'

'None of this is much use if we can't read it,' said Clay.

'Hopefully Mr Symmonds will soon be able to help with that,' said Lord Ringmore.

John Symmonds gave a noncommittal grunt.

'Why thirteen?' asked Sir Tyrrell.

'I don't yet know,' replied Mr G. Hayman. 'Black cats, smashed mirrors, unlucky number thirteen. All of these things have real meaning and *The Book of Thirteen* is our connection to them all.'

'I still haven't heard anything but speculation,' said Clay.

'Which must mean it's your turn to step up, Harry,' said Lord Ringmore. 'While Mr Symmonds is delving into the book's meaning and Mr Hayman continues to search for its place in our history, we need you to investigate the book's qualities and ensure that it is not a fake.'

'With pleasure. Hand it over then,' replied Clay.

'The book is currently under lock and key in my house,' said Lord Ringmore. 'You will accompany me there once our meeting has concluded to collect it. Then you can subject it to your most rigorous investigations.'

'Very well,' said Clay, 'but I warn you, I have never met a medium, magician or conjuror who has been able to convince me of the existence of anything genuinely magical. As you're so enjoying this fantasy of yours, are you sure you want me to shatter it?'

'We seek the truth,' said Lord Ringmore. 'The truth about life, about death and about magic.'

'And what about me?' said Sir Tyrrell. 'You appear to have passed over all researching duties to this novelist.'

'If you wish to help me, Sir Tyrrell,' said Mr G. Hayman, 'I would warmly welcome your involvement. I am to meet one of my interview subjects tomorrow. Perhaps you could join me.'

Sir Tyrrell let out a small harrumph in apparent acceptance of the invitation.

'Excellent. Then we all have our roles,' said Lord Ringmore. 'Every one of us will contribute and every one of us will benefit. We have in our possession a key that will unlock doors you haven't even dared to dream exist. Let us progress wisely.'

14

Betrayal

The orphans looked up at the sliver of light from the gap between the thick velvet curtains of the gentlemen's club study. Had there been time to slip inside, they would be benefitting from the warmth of the fire, but Tom had arrived late so they were stuck out in the cold, listening to each other's chattering teeth.

'What do you think they're talking about?' asked Esther.

'Who cares?' said Tom. 'We need to get our money and move on.'

'Lord Ringmore said there would be more tasks.'

'I say we get out while we're up and leave them to their silly society,' said Tom.

'Are you completely Bedlam?' demanded Esther. 'This is a good thing we're on to.'

'Running around London for a couple of coins whenever Lord Top Hat decides to throw them our way?' said Tom. 'It ain't much better than begging.'

'Don't you want to know about the book though?' said Esther. 'All that stuff we overhead them say before. What if it's true?'

'What? Magic?' scoffed Tom. 'And you call *me* mad!'

'Why not? All them miracles the nuns used to bang on about, what were they if not magic?'

'That's the Bible. It's different,' argued Tom. 'And this business has got nothing to do with us.'

'Since when did we let that get in our way?' asked Esther.

'We have options. There are other ways to get by.'

'What ways? What options?' Esther turned to face Tom. He tried to look away but she refused to let him. She could see he was hiding something. She would find out what if she had to shake it out of him. 'What is it?' she demanded. 'You've been acting odd since this morning. What happened while you were following the Indian?'

'Nothing. Nothing happened.'

'I don't believe you. Tell me what.'

Tom met her gaze. 'All right, so I bumped into Hardy,' he admitted. 'So what?'

'Hardy? What did he do to you?'

'He threatened me is all.'

'But you got away?'

'Yes . . .' Tom hated it when Esther spoke to him as though she was his mother. 'I told him about Ringmore. I couldn't see it would do any harm. I thought it might even make him lay off a bit.'

'Did it?' said Esther.

'It will now. I done a deal, you see,' said Tom. 'I went to

see him again just now. Everything's going to be all right. That's why I was late here.'

'What deal?'

'A deal to keep him off our backs. We'll be safe from him now.'

'What have you done, Tom?'

'I told him about Ringmore's house being empty tonight is all. He'll go and clear it out and we'll get our cut and then he'll leave us alone. You see? I done good, didn't I Est?'

'*Good*?' exclaimed Esther. 'Ringmore will know it was us!'

Tom shrugged. 'So we'll get our money when he comes out here, then disappear. Ringmore won't send the coppers after us. You've seen how secretive he is about everything.'

'We've got to tell him.' Esther made to cross the road but Tom grabbed her hand and dragged her back, almost pulling her arm free from its socket.

'Tell him?' said Tom. 'Have you lost your mind? What are you going to tell him?'

'I'm going to tell him he needs to send the coppers round.'

'You can't. They'll find Hardy there.'

'Good. He deserves to swing.'

'He'll get away. You know he will, Est. Then he'll come looking for us. He'll kill us. There's nothing we can do now. It's done, Est. It's done.'

Esther stared angrily at Tom. She knew he was right. She looked up at the study window where silhouettes shifted behind the thick curtains. 'He trusted us,' she said. 'And you've betrayed him.'

'You seen how quick he was to raise his stick when I asked the wrong question. He's using us and when he's finished he'll throw us to the dogs. We're nothing to him, people like us.'

'You're right. We are nothing, but he was giving us a chance to be something.'

'Chances get taken, not given.'

Esther knew she couldn't win the argument. Tom was too stubborn and it was too late. They had betrayed Lord Ringmore and that was that.

15

Looted

As the hansom cab transported Lord Ringmore and Mr Clay across London, they kept the conversation light and avoided further mention of the book for fear of being overheard. Instead the two men discussed Clay's forthcoming appearance at the Theatre Royal in Victoria, where he was to take to the stage for a solid month of nightly performances. Lord Ringmore expressed doubts that such a long run was wise but Clay explained that they had already sold out the first two weeks and had added the second fortnight due to public demand.

'My stunt on the Thames created some very positive publicity,' said Clay. 'Who needs to pay for expensive advertisements when the columnists of London are so keen to fill their rags with glowing reviews?'

When the cab drew up outside Lord Ringmore's house, he paid the driver and turned to find Clay already standing in front of his door.

'I take it you're in the habit of locking your front door when you leave,' said Clay.

'Of course,' replied Lord Ringmore. 'Why?'

The cab driver whipped his horse and drove away.

'It's open.' Clay pushed the door.

Lord Ringmore smiled. 'It's rather late for your tricks, Harry.'

'Unfortunately this is not a trick. Not one of mine, at least.' Clay stepped over the threshold.

Lord Ringmore rushed up the steps and pushed past him. The whole place had been turned over. Drawers had been pulled out and rifled through. Items collected on his travels that had adorned his shelves and mantelpieces had been removed, but there was only one object that Lord Ringmore cared about. He took the stairs two at a time, not caring when his cloak caught and ripped on an empty hook where an oil painting had hung.

At the top of the stairs he found the door to his upstairs study. From his pocket he drew a key but as his eyes settled on the oak bureau, the key fell to the floor. The bureau's lid had been prized off. It was empty.

Clay stood behind him. 'The book was in there?' he asked, already knowing the answer. 'Any idea who could be behind this? Someone knew you were out.'

'The orphans,' snarled Lord Ringmore.

'You think they came for the book?' asked Clay.

'No. My guess is that these thieves were after the valuables,' said Lord Ringmore. 'But I have no doubt the orphans were involved. The boy asked about my lack of servants.

He saw the opportunity of an empty house. It was my own fault.'

'I can retrieve it for you,' said Clay.

'How can you?' replied Lord Ringmore, feeling all hope drain from him. 'We have lost it. I should never have left it here. I thought it safer than carrying it around. What was I thinking?'

'You can spend your time asking yourself such questions or you can place your faith in me,' replied Clay. 'Mark my words, I will find that book. I know more of these thieves' world than you might expect.'

'You, Harry?'

'I was not born the Remarkable Harry Clay. My beginnings were humble enough. Now, I noticed downstairs a bottle of brandy overlooked by the thieves in their hurry. I think this would be as good a time as any to open it, wouldn't you say?'

16

Bloodstone

Tom and Esther walked in silence to the address off Coldharbour Lane where they were to meet Hardy. Esther was too angry to talk. Working for Lord Ringmore, even for such a short amount of time, had given her a glimpse of another world. Sister Eucharia used to say that God had a plan for everyone. Esther liked that idea. What if Lord Ringmore was that plan for Esther? Hardy hadn't just stolen Lord Ringmore's possessions. He had robbed Tom and Esther of any hopes of a better life.

The house was hidden away under the shadow of a grimy railway bridge that rattled each time a train went over. The orphans stopped under the bridge and looked for signs of life. They had been here once before. The house belonged to a filthy old miser named Max Bloodstone, who exchanged stolen goods for hard cash. Bloodstone wasn't his real name, but he was so called because the chance of getting a fair price from him was often compared to extracting blood from a stone.

'You don't need to come in if you don't want to,' said Tom.

'We may as well get something out of all this,' said Esther.

'I mean, you don't need to come in the house with me. I can go and collect our cut if you like.'

A train rattled past overhead, its clattering carriages shattering the quiet of the night. Tom was Esther's best friend. If she couldn't trust him, who could she trust? She refused to believe that he would take more than his fair share, and yet, Tom had changed in these months since they left the orphanage. He had hardened. The old Tom would never have betrayed her, but she didn't know about this new one.

'Come on, let's get this over with,' she said.

Brewer opened the door to them and smiled. 'Ah, two lost little orphans,' he said.

'We're no less orphans than you,' said Esther.

'And no littler neither,' added Tom.

'You two are still fresh on the street. I've been out here for over a year now.'

'Yeah, well, we still remember those beatings old Mother Agnes used to give you,' said Tom.

'I'd like to see her try that now.' Brewer held his knife up. 'I'd cut her up good and proper. Anyway, you'd better come in. Max don't like people hanging around outside.'

The house was dark and grubby. In a small downstairs room with the curtains drawn, Worms and Stump sat playing cards. Seeing Tom, Stump went to go for him but Hardy appeared at the top of the stairs and said, 'Why, if it ain't Hansel and Gretel?'

'We want our money, Hardy,' said Esther.

'So very blunt,' he replied. 'No nice to see yous. No thanks for what I done for you.'

'What've you done for us?' demanded Tom. 'It was me that told you the house to rob.'

'And it was me what robbed it,' replied Hardy. 'Now come on up and we'll talk cuts.'

Brewer joined the card game and the orphans followed Hardy upstairs into a room where Max Bloodstone sat behind a desk piled high with candlesticks, snuff boxes, ornaments, jewellery, hats, umbrellas and all manner of other items from Lord Ringmore's house. Bloodstone, an old man with more wiry white hair on his chin than on his head, looked up at the orphans with a mistrustful glance.

'I know you,' he snarled.

'These are them orphans I told you about. They're the ones who told me about the place.'

'Good tip-off,' said Bloodstone, begrudgingly. 'All sorts of intriguing objects our lads come back with from that place. Rare, a lot of 'em. Of course, rare often don't make them any easier to sell. '

'So how much, Max?' asked Hardy. 'I said I'd split it fair and square with these two.'

'Five pounds for the lot,' said Bloodstone.

'Five pounds?' exclaimed Esther. 'We cleared out this man's house and you say five pounds?'

'That's two pounds, ten shillings for you two,' said Hardy.

'Come on, Est. That's more money than we've ever had,' said Tom.

'Don't be such an idiot, Tom,' said Esther. 'You see what he's doing? These two have already agreed a price and then he's told him to say something lower for us.'

'You want to be careful what you're saying,' said Bloodstone. 'I always treat my clients fair.'

'That's right,' said Hardy. 'This is business, not one of your street games.'

'It's a good price,' said Tom. 'It'll keep us fed for a while.'

'We sold a man's life for two quid ten?' said Esther.

'You didn't tell me they'd be trouble,' said Bloodstone. 'Hollerin' away like this. You know these walls ain't exactly thick. I can't have no hollerin' in here. You know that, Hardy.'

'There'll be no more trouble, Max.' Hardy turned on the orphans. 'I tell you what, we'll make it three quid and be done.'

'Three quid, Est,' said Tom, pleadingly.

Esther didn't reply. She had noticed a book on the desk amongst the other things. A black scarf prevented her from seeing the whole thing but she could make out the curve of a number three on the cover.

'Three quid is still robbery and no question,' she said. 'But I'll take it if we can have something from the pile too.'

Hardy sniggered. 'It don't work like that. Thieves get their cut then sellers sell the wares.'

'That's right. I've gotta have something to sell, ain't I?' said Bloodstone.

'Only something small,' said Esther. 'Something not worth much.'

'Everything's worth something,' said Bloodstone, gathering the objects on the desk in his arms, protectively.

'What is it you want, out of interest?' asked Hardy, his cold eyes trained on Esther.

Esther shrugged as casually as she could manage then stepped forward. She glanced at the objects on the table, trying to ignore Bloodstone's discouraging grunts every time her eyes settled on something. Her hand moved across the items, picking up a couple of things and examining them with mock interest, until she lifted the scarf off the book and saw the number thirteen on the cover. She could feel Hardy's twitching eyes upon her. She steadied her hand and picked up the book.

'How about this?' she said.

'A book?' sneered Hardy. 'Didn't have you down as a reader, Esther.'

'I just want something to remember this by. It is our biggest robbery, after all,' she replied. 'I don't suppose this old thing is worth much.'

Bloodstone breathed a sigh of relief. 'Oh, she can have the book. I was going to chuck that anyway.'

Hardy leant forward and snatched the book out of Esther's hand.

'Thieves keep mementoes at their peril,' he said.

'Give her the book and let me get back to my work,' snapped Bloodstone.

'I think if she gets what she wants then I should get what

I want.' Hardy turned to face her, holding the book behind his back.

'What would that be?' asked Esther.

'A kiss.' He smiled. 'You give me a little kiss and I'll give you the book.'

'No,' said Tom. 'Leave her alone.'

'I ain't talking to you,' said Hardy, his eyes fixed on Esther. 'Now, what do you say? How badly do you want this memento of yours? Because I know how badly I want that kiss.'

'I'd rather kiss a cockroach,' said Esther.

'None of them around.' Hardy shrugged.

'She isn't going to kiss you,' said Tom. 'Now give us our money and let us go.'

'Give them their cut, Max,' said Hardy. 'But I think I'll keep this book. Maybe next time we meet you'll have changed your mind about that kiss.'

Esther watched helplessly as he slid the book into the inside pocket of his coat.

17

Plan

It was a long way from Bloodstone's dark corner of South London to the orphans' Rotherhithe home but Tom and Esther were used to long walks. In the day they would hitch rides by jumping on the backs of hansom cabs or omnibuses until they were caught and shooed off, but the streets were quiet so late at night and they didn't want to draw any attention to themselves at such a murderous hour. Sometimes they would put their arms around each other to keep warm, but tonight they walked apart in spite of the cold wind.

'You going to stay angry with me?' asked Tom. They had reached the long road that took them through Walworth and would eventually bring them to Elephant and Castle.

'I'm not angry,' said Esther.

'Upset then.'

'When did you decide to go to Hardy?'

'Just seemed like a good idea.'

'It was the reason you suggested we split this evening,

wasn't it?'

'So what if it was?'

'You should have asked me.'

'I knew you'd say no,' admitted Tom. 'But it had to be done, Est. We got Hardy off our backs now.'

'Or more like, he thinks we work for him.'

'Maybe that's not such a bad idea. We got money now, and more than the dribs and drabs old Ringmore was throwing us.'

'You didn't like being bossed around by a toff like that but you don't mind if it's a toerag like Hardy. Is that it?' asked Esther.

'It's different,' replied Tom. 'Hardy comes from the same place as us. Ringmore is never gonna see us as anything but street rats.'

'Not now, he won't,' said Esther, angrily. 'That's for sure.'

'I just thought –'

'You shouldn't,' interrupted Esther. 'You should leave the thinking to me.'

'Why? Because you're cleverer than me? That's what you think, isn't it?'

Esther didn't reply. They fell silent as they passed a pub, lively with the sounds of voices raised in drunken singing.

'You and me, Tom,' said Esther. 'We're the only family we got.'

'I'm not like you. I got a family,' said Tom. 'My aunt –'

'Your aunt left you, Tom,' snapped Esther.

'Only 'cos she had to. She had no choice. She never wanted to leave me at that place. You'll see. One day I'll be able to find her again and then you'll see. I know she's out there, Est. I know she is.'

'How you going to find her?'

'When I've got money. Money can get you anything you want.'

'If it's money you want you'll help me get that book off Hardy.'

'Can't we just forget about that stupid book now? You don't believe it's actually magic, do you?'

'It's not important what I believe. What's important is that Ringmore believes it.'

'What you on about?'

'You want money and Ringmore will do anything to get the book back. He'll pay anything to get it back.'

Tom looked at her and, for the first time since they had set off, smiled. 'You think he will?'

'Real, make-a-difference money, Tom. No matter what I believe, it's worth it for that, ain't it?'

'But Hardy's got it in his coat pocket and I've never even seen him take that coat off. Maybe we should buy the book back off him.'

'No. He mustn't know how much we want it. He already thinks there's something up with it because of what happened back at Bloodstone's. We need to get it from him without him knowing it was us what took it.'

'I don't fancy pickpocketing Hardy.'

'Don't worry. I've got an idea. We'll swipe it right from under his nose.'

'He'll kill us if he catches us.'

'This idea I got, he won't even know it was us.'
'I'm listening.'
'Friday's collection day,' said Esther. 'Except this Friday it won't just be Hardy who's collecting.'

18

Investigations

Lord Ringmore was impressed with Clay's skills of detection. He had an uncanny ability to extract information from his interviewees, often without them knowing they were the subjects of an interrogation at all. By the end of the first day, having mixed with some of London's most despicable characters and visited some of the city's most deprived areas, Clay had established that Tom and Esther had begun life at an orphanage in Southwark by the name of St Clement's Catholic School for Waifs and Strays.

Lord Ringmore had been most insistent that they conduct the investigation together, even if he had so far done little more than observe. As the two men walked briskly across London Bridge, Clay explained how he'd first discovered his natural flair for investigation.

'A couple of years back, I was touring America; working the backwaters, you know, the small towns,' said Clay. 'I was in one of these towns when I read in some local rag about an abduction of a young girl. Reading the details, it occurred to me that if I were able to discover the culprit myself then I could use this information in my performance.'

'Use it how?' asked Lord Ringmore.

Clay adopted a distinctly sheepish demeanour. 'I was still doing the medium stuff back then. I thought that if I knew the whereabouts of this child I could appear to draw the answer from the spiritual world as part of the act.'

'Did it work?'

'Like a dream. It wasn't so hard to discover the truth of the abduction. In fact, she had run off with her cousin. That night, I made it seem that the mysterious forces of the universe revealed her whereabouts to me. The young girl was recovered and I was proclaimed the hero.'

'All this from Harry Clay, the scourge of false mediums.'

'Yeah, well, we've all got skeletons, haven't we, Ringmore? Besides, my methods may have been questionable but my conclusion was sound. So I started doing the same in every town I visited. It made for an excellent aspect of the show, but more importantly it made the newspapers.'

'And of course, you solved these crimes,' added Lord Ringmore.

'And that, yes,' replied Clay, dismissively. 'In Connecticut, I even got a murder inquiry reopened and the guilty party arrested, tried and hanged. That made it all the way to New York. Journalists everywhere picked up on it. It was well worth the death threats from the relatives of the culprit. Well worth it. I was dining out on that one for months.'

In spite of their differences of background and opinion, conversation always ran easily between Lord Ringmore and Harry Clay. But both men fell silent when they reached the imposing red-brick orphanage in Southwark.

'You began life in a similar institution, did you not, Harry?' asked Lord Ringmore.

Clay nodded. 'It's different when you look back on it,' he said. 'You can remember the details – you know, the smells, the sounds – but you forget the despair. It's like pain. You can remember that you felt it but you can't bring to mind exactly *how* it felt.'

'Then you should be grateful that the pain has subsided,' said Lord Ringmore.

A pug-faced nun opened the excessively bolted door. Clay explained that they desired a brief interview with the prioress, regarding funding, and the nun led them down a corridor that smelt of boiled cabbage and body odour. In her office, Mother Agnes, the prioress, greeted them unsmilingly, demonstrating no recognition of Clay's celebrity when he gave his name.

'And what can I do for you two gentlemen?' she asked coldly.

'We are in search of a pair of orphans,' replied Lord Ringmore.

'We have more than our fair share of those,' said the nun.

'They go by the names Tom and Esther,' he explained.

'I would have to check our ledger. We have a good many orphans through these doors with a good many names. What, may I ask, is your interest in them? If you claim parentage, I should warn you that it will prove costly to extract them from the system. We are a sanctuary for lost souls, not a pawnbroker for children.'

Clay placed a hand on Lord Ringmore's arm, indicating that he should let him take the lead. 'Mother Agnes, I grew up in an institution like this,' he said. 'And since becoming a man of means, I have gained something of a reputation for generosity in supporting such places . . . financially. Sometimes I am too generous. My friend is here to ensure that I don't write a cheque so big as to ruin myself.'

The meanest of smiles broke out on the nun's pale face. It sat there both unnaturally and, if the pained look in her eyes was anything to go by, uncomfortably.

'The Lord knows this charitable institution needs all the financial help it can get. You are a Catholic yourself, Mr Clay?'

'By inclination if not by birth,' replied Clay, vaguely. 'Will you check your ledger?'

'Now I think about it, I believe I do remember these two you speak of. Sadly, they are no longer here. They were taken.'

'Taken?' said Lord Ringmore.

'By the devil. He leads many of our children away. He tempts them into lives of thieves and vagabonds. We try to steer them along the correct path, but Lucifer can be far more enticing to young minds. And I'm sorry to say that these two always had him in their hearts. Thomas had potential but he was led astray by the girl, who was born with Satan inside her.'

'You think a child can be born with the devil in its heart?' said Clay.

'I have seen it many times. The boy, he was weak. He had an unhealthy belief that one day his family would return for him.'

'What was he doing here if he had family?' asked Lord Ringmore.

'His parents were both dead. He was brought here by an aunt. He was convinced that she would return for him one day, but they never do. It was not hard for the girl to lead him from this sanctuary into the world of sin.'

'How long ago did they leave?' asked Clay.

'Six months ago.'

'Do you know where they are now?'

'Paying rent to the devil, no doubt.'

Clay reached into his inside pocket and pulled out a cheque book. 'I would like to make a contribution,' he said, 'but I do need to find these two orphans. Any ideas where I might look?'

The nun met his gaze. 'You might want to try Holborn. They wouldn't be the first of our former pupils to end up running those streets. But please, can you tell me why you are seeking them?'

Neither man answered, not wanting to add credence to this foul woman's beliefs. 'We seek their salvation,' said Lord Ringmore at last.

'Then I fear a hopeless quest lies ahead of you,' said Mother Agnes. 'Some are beyond saving.'

19

Swiped

On collection days Hardy would extract money from the shopkeepers of Holborn in exchange for protection from the many nefarious types who operated in that area. He liked interacting with honest business folk and, on the whole, they dealt with him respectfully. No one wanted to make a fuss. For one day a week, Hardy felt like he was a part of the community. He always left the other boys outside the shops when he went in, but they were on hand if there was any trouble or if the shopkeepers needed reminding of what exactly they were paying to be protected from.

Hardy stepped into Mr Pryce's bakery and was instantly hit by the delicious smell of warm bread. It was warm inside so he undid the two top buttons of his coat. It was crowded too, with customers queuing up in front of the counter, jostling for position, but Mr Pryce clocked Hardy as soon as he entered and immediately broke off from serving a tall lady in a bright blue coat.

'Hey, there's a queue here,' said one of the customers.

'That's right,' said the lady in the blue coat. 'Mr Pryce was taking my order.'

'I'm sorry,' replied the baker, 'but this is an urgent matter. My assistant will finish off your order.'

'More urgent than a paying customer?' proclaimed the lady, turning her head to see the cause of this interruption.

Hardy smiled, revealing his brown teeth.

Some of the customers recognised him and looked away but this lady obviously had no idea who he was.

'I'm sure this young man won't mind waiting his turn,' she said.

Hardy hated people talking about him like he wasn't there.

'This gentleman is collecting a pre-order for his master,' said Mr Pryce, hastily. 'It won't take a moment and, in the meantime, my assistant will continue to serve you.'

Hardy did not appreciate the demotion to servitude in Mr Pryce's invented story. The blue-coated lady scowled at him. Mr Pryce pulled out from under the counter a batch of rolls, in which the payment was secreted. He attempted to hand it to Hardy, but another voice piped up. 'He's pushing in.'

'Yes. There are others here, you know,' said someone else.

'Quite,' said the blue-coated lady, who seemed more interested in Hardy than in the assistant who was desperately trying to help her with her order.

More faces turned to look at him in anger and disapproval. Hardy didn't like the odds. In his experience people were easy to intimidate one to one, but standing together, united against him, he was vastly outnumbered. This wasn't how it was supposed to work.

He pushed his way through the disgruntled rabble to grab the batch of rolls from Mr Pryce but, as he did so, he failed to notice a passing boy who was carrying a large bag of flour above his head and had his cap pulled over his face. As Hardy collided with the lad, the bag went flying upwards, spraying its powdery contents into the air. Hardy felt the lad tug at his coat to steady himself and angrily batted him away. He snatched the rolls from Mr Pryce and left the shop.

Outside, Brewer, Worms and Stump were standing with their backs to the window. They turned to face Hardy, who was now covered in white powder.

'What happened to you?' asked Brewer.

'If you'd been doing your jobs you'd know exactly what happened to me,' said Hardy.

'Why are you all white?' said Stump.

'It's flour, you idiot,' snapped Hardy. He threw the batch of rolls at him. 'Come on.'

They started to walk away, but behind them the bakery door opened again and the lady with the blue coat cried, 'Thief! Stop that man. He stole my purse!'

Hardy turned around. 'Listen lady,' he began, but as he did so he sunk his hands into his pockets and felt something unfamiliar. He pulled out the lady's purse.

Hardy would have thrown the blasted thing in her face except that the lady's hysterical cries had attracted the attention of a nearby policeman, who was now running towards them, sounding his shrill whistle.

'Run!' said Hardy.

The others did not need to be told twice. They turned tail and fled as the copper charged after them. The usual procedure was to split up, so Brewer and Stump headed towards Holborn Viaduct, while Hardy and Worms ran down Southampton Row, but the trail of white flour from Hardy's coat meant the copper stayed with them.

When they took another corner, a second policeman caught on to the commotion and joined in the chase.

'Come on.' Hardy booted over an applecart to slow down the coppers and dragged Worms into an alleyway.

'Give me your coat,' Hardy said, hastily removing his own.

'Eh?'

'Don't argue. You're a faster runner than me. Swap coats.'

Hardy was not going to wait for permission. He yanked Worms's coat and handed him his own, ordering him to put it on. With the coats swapped, they continued to the end of the alleyway. The two coppers had got past the applecart and had them in their sights again.

'You go that way,' ordered Hardy. 'Meet back at the usual place.'

As the two coppers emerged from the alleyway, they paused a moment but, seeing the trail of flour, took off after Worms.

Worms picked up his pace. With his long legs and lean figure, he could outrun the best of them. It wasn't long before he could hear the two coppers panting. Worms took a route through the middle of Bloomsbury Square Gardens. He leapt over the surrounding fence and sprinted across the grass, but caught his foot on something and tripped, tumbling over and landing on his back.

'Quick, get up.' Tom's face loomed over him. He held a hand out and pulled him up.

'Cheers, mate,' said Worms, confused but grateful for the help. He sprang to his feet then continued on his way. Even with the setback of a fall, it only took another couple of corners for him to lose the coppers. Once he could no longer see them, he slowed to a walk and took cover behind a wall to check behind him and ensure they weren't still nearby, as Hardy had always told him to. Finally, sure he had lost them, he headed back to the gang's current meeting spot, a secluded alleyway off Museum Street.

The other three were already there when he arrived. Hardy had removed Worms' coat and was holding it at arm's length.

'Took your time, didn't you?' he said. 'Now give me back my coat. Yours stinks.'

Worms reached to take his coat but Hardy dropped it on the ground. It landed in a puddle. The others laughed. Worms picked it up and handed Hardy's back to him.

Hardy dusted it down. 'I'll have to get this cleaned now it's been on your sweaty back,' he grumbled, pulling it on and doing it up. 'Hey, where's the book?'

'What book?' asked Worms.

'The one in the inside pocket,' replied Hardy. 'The one that orphan girl wanted. Where's the book?'

'I don't know nothing about no book,' replied Worms.

'It was there when we swapped coats.'

'I suppose it could've fallen out when I tripped.'

'Where did you trip?'

'In the park back there. Tom helped me back up.'

'Did he indeed?' snarled Hardy. 'Come on.'

20

Creation

Tom and Esther had agreed to head straight back to Rotherhithe as soon as one of them had retrieved the book, but Tom lingered for a moment under the tree in the centre of Bloomsbury Square Gardens, ensuring that none of Hardy's gang was still in the vicinity. The plan had involved Hardy ditching his coat altogether. When he had swapped it instead, Tom had been forced to trip Worms and take the book from him, but now he was worried that Hardy could too easily connect Tom's appearance with the missing book.

While he waited, he opened the book and looked at the intricately drawn shapes that filled its pages, wondering what they meant. A movement in the tree caught his eye and he saw he was not alone. A magpie hopped along the branch, looking at him, twitching its head. Its tattered feathers revealed patchy, pink skin underneath. One eye hung out of its socket.

'Clear off,' said Tom.

The magpie swooped down to the ground and picked up a twig in its beak. It walked forward then dropped it at Tom's feet. Tom had never seen a bird act in such a way.

'What do you want?' asked Tom.

The magpie hopped back. Tom picked up the twig. The bird flapped its wings excitedly, causing feathers to come loose and flutter to the ground.

'I don't understand,' said Tom.

The disgusting creature flew at him. Tom recoiled in revulsion and dropped the book while trying to bat it away. The magpie landed in front of the book and tapped its beak on the back cover. On it was a circle within a triangle within a larger circle. The magpie tapped its beak on the shape, nodded at Tom, then tapped the ground.

'You want me to draw this shape in the ground?' Now he was talking to a bird. Tom wondered what the chances were that he had gone mad.

The magpie nodded. Tom knew perfectly well that magpies did not nod in response to questions.

'Can you understand me?' said Tom.

Again, the magpie nodded.

'And you want me to draw this shape on the ground with this twig?'

The magpie flew up to the branch again and tapped its beak on the bark. Mad or not, Tom understood that the bird wanted him to break off a larger branch. He dropped the twig and chose a good, sizable branch about the same length as his own arm. He jumped up and pulled it from the tree. It came free with a clean break. He pulled off a couple of smaller offshoots while the magpie impatiently tapped the ground.

'Hold your horses, will you?' said Tom. He peered down at the book and studied the shape then dug the twig into the ground and did his best to recreate it.

'There,' he said.

But the magpie was not happy. It flapped its wings and flew round and round his head, its disgustingly grubby wings brushing against his face.

'What?' said Tom, batting it away.

Once again the magpie flew round and round in circles.

'You want me to draw it bigger?' guessed Tom.

The magpie nodded.

Tom drew the shape again. When it was complete the magpie tapped the middle of the shape on the book. Tom understood that he was supposed to stand in the centre of the shape. With the stick still in his hand, Tom stepped inside, placing both feet within the smaller of the two circles.

He felt a strange sensation. At first it was as though he was being swallowed up by the ground. Then it was more like the ground was raising him up. The three shapes, which had barely been visible on the cold, hard ground, grew distinct. Tom felt the beauty of their symmetry. He saw shapes in everything he looked at. They were there in the grey sky divided by the leafless branches of the tree. He saw them in the blades of grass and the bark of the tree. Colours deepened. Browns and greens spread up from the soil and stained his feet, creeping up his body. His own hands aged in front of his eyes. His heartbeat quickened. Tom felt power and strength like he had never felt before. Then, whatever had him in its grip released him and he collapsed to the ground.

'At last,' said a voice. 'I thought I was going to have to spend all day hopping about, tapping this withered old beak like a demented bird.'

Tom lifted his head and looked at the mangy magpie.

'You can talk?' he said.

'The point is not that I can talk but that you are finally able to listen,' said the magpie.

Yes, thought Tom. This was most definitely madness.

21

Mavis

Following Mr G. Hayman off the train, Sir Tyrrell found his mind wandering back to his constituency meeting and the troubling lady who had been so vocal in her support of votes for women. There was no question that the world was changing. Sir Tyrrell was by no means against progress but the future represented by these modern women troubled him deeply. This fine old country needed fine old men like him to uphold the values that had ensured its greatness for so many centuries, but it sometimes seemed to him that he was part of a dying breed in politics. There were too many young men with new ideas, when what the world really required was stability.

'This had better be worth our while. I'm missing an important parliamentary debate for this,' he grumbled, as they walked through the quiet Kent village.

'There is never any guarantee that these research trips will be fruitful,' said Mr G. Hayman. 'But I have interviewed

Mavis before and she has much to say.'

Sir Tyrrell grunted but made no further comment. Mr G. Hayman led them to a cottage with wild green vines growing over its walls, as though the earth itself was rising up and slowly devouring it.

To Sir Tyrrell's eyes the old woman who answered the door looked like the epitome of what a witch should look like. Had she lived a hundred years ago, she would undoubtedly have found herself on the wrong side of a pitchfork and an angry mob. The crooked nose and hairy warts were straight out of an illustrated version of *Macbeth* that Sir Tyrrell had owned as a child, and yet her eyes twinkled kindly as she welcomed them into her home.

'Hello, Mavis,' said Mr G. Hayman. 'I came to see you on a previous occasion. My name is –'

'Georgina,' interrupted the old woman. 'Yes, I remember you. Come in, my dear. You have a friend this time.'

'This is Sir –' began Mr G. Hayman.

'Augustus will do,' interrupted Sir Tyrrell hastily.

'Pleased to meet you,' said Mavis, leading them into a cosy but dimly lit room. Sir Tyrrell took Mr G. Hayman's lead in accepting a cup of tea, although he had his doubts about the cleanliness of the cup in which it was served.

'So what would you like to know about?' asked Mavis.

'*The Book of Thirteen*,' said Mr G. Hayman. 'You told me about it last time I visited.'

'Ah yes, Olwyn Broe's book.'

'What do you know about it?' asked Mr G. Hayman.

'It was Olwyn's spell book, so they say.'

'A spell book with no words?' said Sir Tyrrell.

The old woman peered at him with renewed interest. 'Why do you say it has no words?' she asked. '*The Book of Thirteen* has not been seen for centuries.'

Unsure how to respond, Sir Tyrrell said nothing.

'When was it written?' asked Mr G. Hayman.

'It was written in the time before Conjury vanished from the world, many centuries ago.'

'Conjury?' said Sir Tyrrell.

'Magic, to you and me,' said Mavis. 'They say that Olwyn knew that Conjury was vanishing and so she wrote down all of her spells.'

'For what reason?' asked Mr G. Hayman.

Mavis nodded. 'Yes, that's the question, isn't it? Why? What was it for? *Who* was it for?'

'And the answers to those questions?' said Sir Tyrrell, impatiently.

'I'm afraid I don't know,' said Mavis.

'Then what is the point of all these riddles?' demanded Sir Tyrrell.

'Sometimes riddles are all we have to remember the past,' said Mavis.

'But what happened to the Conjurors? Why did Conjury disappear?' asked Sir Tyrrell.

Mavis sipped her tea. 'While Olwyn was writing her book, there was another force tearing through the land, destroying the Conjurors.'

'You speak of witch-hunters,' said Sir Tyrrell.

'They took their share, it's true, but they alone could not

have wiped out the Conjurors. No, it was one of their own who sealed their fate. A Conjuror by the name of Mondriat, who wanted to make himself more powerful, set about stealing Conjury and obliterating his own kind, one by one.'

'Did he also kill Olwyn?' asked Mr G. Hayman.

'No,' said Mavis. 'There was something between them. When he was done, they were the last two remaining, but even Conjurors cannot cheat the reaper and their deaths brought the end of Conjury. Perhaps Olwyn wrote the book so there was something to remember them by, but it has not been seen since her death.'

'So why thirteen?' asked Mr G. Hayman. 'What does it mean?'

Mavis put her teacup down. 'It is said only a thirteen-year-old can become a Conjuror.'

'A child?' barked Sir Tyrrell.

The old woman nodded. 'Only a thirteen-year-old has the strength to endure the process of drawing in the lifeblood, while possessing a mind still open to the infinite possibilities of Conjury.'

'Are you saying that any thirteen-year-old can perform magic?' said Sir Tyrrell.

'No, not any,' said Mavis. 'Conjurors are children of the Earthsoul. Therefore they must be alone in the world.'

'Orphaned?' said Mr G. Hayman.

'That's it.' She nodded.

'There are enough thirteen-year-old orphans in the world,' said Sir Tyrrell. 'Why are none of them Conjurors any more?'

'Because the old ways have been forgotten,' replied Mavis.

'One must know how to perform the Creation Spell to become Infected.'

Sir Tyrrell looked at Mr G. Hayman. He had interviewed his fair share of experts and was as adept as any at picking out the frauds and the deluded. Mavis struck him as neither. Right or wrong, he was in no doubt that she believed every word.

22

Cards

Esther stared out at the river. She was worried. Tom should have been back at the warehouse by now. Even if something had gone wrong and he had failed to snatch the book, he should have come back. Esther was staring so intently into the darkness that she nearly jumped out of her skin when a quiet meow from the window signalled the arrival of a black cat. She wondered whether it could possibly be the same one she had seen outside Mr Symmonds' house.

'Hello puss,' she said.

The cat stepped down onto the mattress. Esther stroked its back, while her mind ran through every possible reason for Tom's absence. None of them was reassuring but one in particular scared her more than the others. Although Esther was only a couple of months older than Tom, she had looked out for him since his first day at the orphanage. It had been her idea to leave and make a life of their own on the streets. If Esther acted as a mother to him then it stood to reason that a time would come when he outgrew her and left her to make his own life, just as they had both outgrown the orphanage.

The creak of a floorboard snapped her out of her thoughts. Someone was inside the building, and it wasn't Tom. He always came in around the outside of the building. This intruder was coming through the inside, jumping up onto the upper floor.

'Who's there?' Esther pushed the cat off her lap and picked up the piece of wood with nails in one end that she kept by the side of her bed.

'I'm not surprised you don't get many guests if you give them all such a welcome.' Harry Clay stepped into the room.

'Why are you here?' demanded Esther.

'I wanted to congratulate you on an excellent performance today at the bakery. Some of the best misdirection work I've ever witnessed.'

'I didn't see you there,' replied Esther.

'No more than your mark saw you dressed up as a baker's boy,' said Clay. 'There's a lot of not being seen today, but it's what people like you and me are good at, isn't it? That's why I had to leave Ringmore out of this one. He's a smart fellow, but he sticks out like a sore thumb.'

'A sore thumb in a top hat,' said Esther.

'Exactly. However, I'm not hiding now and we can see each other clearly.' He held out his open palms.

'I don't know what you want.'

'Isn't it obvious?' said Clay. 'The same thing you wanted when you did your whole flour-throwing act. I want the book, Esther.'

'I haven't a clue what you're talking about.'

'Let's drop all the lies now, shall we?' said Clay.

'I haven't got it.'

'Of course not. When you failed to make a straight snatch in the shop you used the flour and planted the purse so your target would ditch it. I'm guessing it was Tom's job to get it if that happened. You were the distraction. Tom was picking up the book, wasn't he? So what shall we do while we wait for him to arrive?' He pulled out a pack of cards. 'You play?'

'You can't just break into people's homes and expect them to play cards with you.'

Mr Clay laughed. It was rich, warm, genuine laughter and it made Esther feel sick to the soles of her feet.

23

Vanishing

Shortly after Tom and Esther ran away from the orphanage they had met an old woman by the name of Mrs Drew who lived in Whitechapel. She was kind to them, even if she did engage in long conversations with her bottle of gin, which she called *my lovely.* She offered them a place to stay for the night, but late that night she crept into their room, holding her gin bottle in one hand and a bread knife in the other. It was lucky Tom had been unable to sleep. As they ran from that house, they heard her calling after them, '*It's not me. I do only that which my lovely bids me do.*' The orphans had laughed about it afterwards, but Tom had wondered since then how easy it was to lose a sense of what was real and what was not. A talking bird, he feared, would have seemed perfectly normal to mad old Mrs Drew.

'You're a talking magpie.' It was all Tom could think to say.

The magpie sighed and looked exasperated. Tom had

never seen a magpie do either of these things before. 'The fact that I can talk should tell you that I am not a magpie at all.'

'You look like a magpie.'

'Of course I look like a magpie,' snapped the bird. 'But was I born a magpie? No, I was not. My name is Mondriat and I was born in Venice, Italy, a long time ago.'

'You don't sound Italian.'

'And you'd be the expert on what an Italian-born Conjuror confined to the body of a magpie should sound like, would you?' retorted the magpie.

'A Conjuror?' whispered Tom.

'A Conjuror,' said the magpie. 'It is what you are. You have been Infected by the lifeblood, the source of energy that flows from the heart of the earth. Can't you feel it flowing through your veins just as it flows through the rivers of the world? The world looks different now, does it not?'

It was true. Every detail was sharper. The rustle of the trees, the movement of the clouds, the sound of earthworms squirming beneath the soil, all of it was so vivid. The world moved so slowly. Or was it him that was moving quickly? Tom took a deep breath and tasted every particle of air. He felt strong. Powerful.

'There is much you need to learn,' said the magpie. 'Much I will tell you. All you need to know now is that you have performed the Creation Spell. The circle encompasses the triangle which holds the circle. These shapes are the basis of all Conjury. Your staff formed the shapes and so you drew the lifeblood into your veins.'

'My staff?' said Tom, looking at the stick he was holding.

'Trees draw straight from the Earthsoul, as does everything that grows from the earth. Any branch may be used but you will find a special affinity for this, your creation staff. In your right hand, your staff must form the spells on the ground, channelling, harnessing, Conjuring that energy while your left turns it into wondrous, beautiful things.'

'Don't I need to say magic words or something?'

'Ridiculous boy,' snorted Mondriat. 'Try shouting at the waves or asking the sun not to set. No, words will not help you.'

'Can you do all these things?'

Mondriat shook his head. 'It takes a human form to draw out the required energy. I am able to overcome these weak animal spirits and squeeze my own into their bodies but a human is a more complex machine. My Conjuring days are behind me but now you have performed the spell I can act as your familiar and together we can bring Conjury back to the world.' Mondriat fluttered up to a high branch. 'Talking of which . . .'

Tom turned to see Hardy and the others walking fast towards them.

'What do I do?' he asked.

'Best to avoid complex spells until you find a mirror.' Mondriat flapped back to the ground, nudged the book open with his beak and flicked through. 'But you could try this one.'

'Try what one?' said Tom.

'Make this spell with your staff,' explained Mondriat,

sounding extremely exasperated.

Tom picked up the book and looked at a picture of two circles inside a larger one with three lines connecting them together. He drew the shape on the ground.

'Now step inside and imagine yourself invisible as the air,' said Mondriat. 'Use the power of the Earthsoul to fuel your imagination.'

Hardy was getting nearer.

'That's it,' continued the magpie. 'Use your other hand to draw the energy around you.'

'It was up here he tripped me,' Worms was saying.

'I think I see someone,' said Brewer.

'Clear your mind. Anything within the realms of your imagination is possible,' said Mondriat.

Hardy appeared around the side of a tree and stopped in front of Tom.

Tom stared back at him. He could see the fury in Hardy's eyes. He wondered why he had decided to listen to the magpie. He should have run. He was about to say something when he realised that Hardy wasn't looking at him. Even though he was standing inches away from his face, Hardy was staring straight through him. He turned to Worms. 'Well, he's not here now.'

'What's so special about that book anyway?' asked Stump.

'That is a very good question,' replied Hardy. 'I think we'd better go and find out, and luckily I know just where to look.'

24

Tricked

Esther remembered how one of the punters on Albert Dock had suggested that Clay had telepathic powers, but she had seen too much trickery and deception on London's streets not to recognise that he was an expert trickster, even when he was putting his skills to grander use. She did not believe for one moment that Clay possessed actual magical powers, but there was something unnerving about his manner as he sat on Tom's mattress, his knowing eyes watching her.

'How do you escape from all them chains then?' she asked.

'I go to great lengths to avoid anyone learning how,' he replied. 'As we say in our industry, reveal the how and lose the wow.'

'You mean that if your audience saw all them trick knots and weak chain links they wouldn't be so keen to throw their hard-earned cash at you?'

Clay smiled. 'You're an intelligent girl. In a few years'

time you come find me and I'll see if I can't fix you up as a magician's assistant.'

'Is that what you are then? A magician?' Esther stroked the black cat, curled up on her lap and softly purring.

'Escapology, mind-reading, spirit-talking, sawing ladies in half,' said Clay. 'It's all trickery, and we tricksters like to call ourselves magicians because, as you rightly point out, it makes it easier to get people to part with their hard-earned money.'

'It's not real magic though, is it?' said Esther.

Clay's gaze seemed to intensify as he leant forward to scrutinise Esther. In his hand he shuffled the pack of cards. He opened them into a fan and offered them to her. 'Take one,' he said.

Esther chose her card carefully, ensuring not to pick one from the side he offered her. She looked at the card. It was the queen of spades.

'Do you think I know your card yet?' he asked.

'Not unless it's a trick pack.'

He turned the pack over to prove that it was not. He flipped it back over, straightened them and told her to push her card into the pack.

'What about now?' he asked. 'Do you think I snuck a peak then?'

'I can't see that you could have,' said Esther.

Clay shuffled the cards then handed her the pack. 'Give it a tap,' he said

Esther did so.

'What are the chances of your card being on top?' he asked.

'Given your job I'd say pretty high,' replied Esther.

'Have a look.'

She turned over the top card. It was the king of spades. She smiled. 'Don't be too hard on yourself,' she said. 'That was pretty close.'

'Very kind of you,' said Clay. 'That was the best I could do, since you have the king's good lady wife tucked under your leg.'

Esther smiled and pulled out the card she had hidden away. 'You saw me do it,' she said. 'You knew I took two cards?'

'Do you know what they used to call those who claimed to have magic? They used to be known as cunning men. If you ask me, this is precisely what they were. Cunning men, conning men. It is all the same. Conjurors of old were nothing more than criminals who would pray on the weak-minded and exploit the confidence they gained for money.'

'So you don't believe in magic at all?'

Clay smiled. 'There have always been people desperate to believe in things they cannot see. Why do you think the church is so wealthy?'

'You ain't short of a few bob yourself,' said Esther.

'I make no claim of having special powers,' said Clay. 'Those who watch my act get what they pay for. They get a spectacle. They get lifted up out of their ordinary lives and shown that the world is a truly amazing place. Not because of magic, but because humans are amazing. My audience doesn't have to convert to a religion or pray to a god and they don't have to wait for death before they are rewarded. They don't have to pay to have fake conversations with dead relatives. When you pay to see Harry Clay, you pay to have your world widened.'

'It's still tricking people for money.'

Clay laughed. 'Too true. We're not so different, then, are we?'

25

Mirrors

With Hardy gone, Tom felt the power that had taken hold of his body suddenly drain away. His head was spinning. He felt weak. He placed a hand on a tree to steady himself but, as his palm connected with the rough bark, he felt a jab of pain and saw a bulbous wart appear on the back of his hand.

'What's happening to me?' he asked.

'The lifeblood's bubbling to the surface. It wants to return to its source.' Mondriat fluttered down to the ground. 'Don't worry. That wart will go down once you have found a mirror.'

'What do I need a mirror for?' asked Tom.

Mondriat hopped along the ground and looked up at him. 'You must cast your True Reflection in order to anchor your spirit to the world.'

'I've got to go and help Esther, first.'

'No, no, no. The Mirror Spell is your priority.' Mondriat

flew around Tom's head, his grabbing wings brushing his face.

'Oi, watch it!' Tom batted him away. 'Esther's my friend and Hardy knows where she is. I need to warn her. Hey, I'll bet I can magic myself there, can't I?'

'You're not listening. No more Conjury until you have found a mirror,' stated Mondriat.

Tom knew he needed to help Esther but the pulsating wart on the back of his hand was an alarming reminder that he should listen to Mondriat.

'If you continue to cast spells untethered you will Conjure yourself into an early grave,' warned the magpie. 'If you must help your friend, do it in a manner that will not put yourself in the way of conflict.'

'There is one way,' said Tom, thinking of Esther's warning system of lighting a fire on the north bank.

'Then do that,' said Mondriat. 'But please promise me, no more spells. Not until –'

'Yeah, yeah, not until I find a mirror. Come on then.'

The winter sky was darkening as Tom arrived on the main thoroughfare with Mondriat perched on his shoulder. An omnibus pulled by two piebald horses was coming down New Oxford Street, making slow progress along the busy road. Tom stopped on a corner to wait for it. He noticed a street trickster by the name of Gibbens, challenging passers-by to identify which of the three thimbles on the table in front of him contained the pea. Several punters stood around him, placing bets. Tom had seen the act before and had always known there was some trick, but now, with eyes so much sharper than before, it was laughably obvious when Gibbens slipped the pea under his long, grubby thumbnail.

Tom felt Mondriat twitching anxiously on his shoulder. Surely one little spell wouldn't hurt. The urge was too strong. Tom moved his staff across the ground, instinctively knowing which shapes would draw the energy to create his desired spell. When Gibbens lifted the chosen thimble he was confused to discover that the pea was no longer under his thumbnail but had somehow shifted to the selected thimble.

'What on earth are you playing at?' cried Mondriat, realising what he had done.

Although Tom was the only one who could understand Mondriat, the squawking magpie on his shoulder was enough to draw several glances. Tom felt a twinge of pain, as though he was being bitten from the inside, and another wart sprang up on his wrist.

'No more Conjury,' ordered Mondriat. 'And look, you've missed the bus now.'

'Don't worry. I'll catch that,' muttered Tom.

Tom had to run full pelt to catch the bus, forcing Mondriat off his shoulder. Leaping over a puddle, he jumped up onto the back and clung on. Mondriat landed on the top deck and peered over the edge.

'Honestly,' he said, shaking his head. 'I've waited hundreds of years for someone who can understand me. Can you imagine how frustrating it is when you don't listen?'

26

Power

In spite of the privileges afforded by his title, Lord Ringmore was not one of Parliament's most regular attendees. The business of government held precious little interest for him, but he knew his way around the corridors of power well enough to locate Sir Tyrrell's private office. As a high-ranking member of the government, Sir Tyrrell had a well-appointed room, overlooking the River Thames. The river looked uninvitingly grey in the low dusk light as Lord Ringmore entered and took a seat opposite. He glanced at the important-looking documents and official dossiers on the desk.

'Working late, Augustus?'

'There is a debate on sewage and sanitation tomorrow so, yes, I have a fair amount to wade through,' said Sir Tyrrell. 'Now what can I do for you?'

'The book has been taken,' replied Lord Ringmore.

'*Taken*? What do you mean, taken?'

'There was a break-in. We believe the orphans have it.'

'We?'

'Clay was there when I discovered it gone.'

'I wouldn't put it past a man like Clay to have stolen it.' Sir Tyrrell picked up a silver pen and waved it reproachfully at Lord Ringmore.

'Your suspicions are misplaced,' insisted Lord Ringmore. 'Clay has been proving very helpful tracking them down.'

'So why are you telling me?' demanded Sir Tyrrell, grumpily.

'I said before that each Society member has a role to play and now is that time.'

Sir Tyrrell put the pen down and leaned forward. 'What role would that be?'

'Reclamation of the book is imperative,' said Lord Ringmore. 'You have a great deal of influence in the city. I believe the Chief Commissioner answers directly to you. The police force would be a great asset to us at this stage.'

'It's out of the question,' barked Sir Tyrrell. 'It would be an abuse of my position.' He sat back in his seat and folded his arms.

'*The exploration of the unknown is an absolute necessity in an ever-changing world*?'

'Fine words but –'

'They were not mine,' said Lord Ringmore. 'You spoke them during a debate on spiritualism. It was the first time we met. We have come a long way since then, you and I, and we are so close to our goal now. We must keep our resolve.'

'There is a big difference between ideology and reality,' said Sir Tyrrell.

'What you mean is that now you hold a position of power, your views have changed.'

Sir Tyrrell sighed. 'Silas, what you're asking is too much.'

'The Society of Thirteen needs your help.'

Sir Tyrrell snorted derisively. 'Finally, I see the reason you've been stringing me along. There I was, thinking you wanted me in this Society of yours because of my expertise in the matters of spiritualism and mysticism. In truth, you asked me because of my governmental position.'

'I understand that you are upset because I gave the book to John first,' said Lord Ringmore.

'Well, I ask you, what knowledge does Symmonds have of these things? A linguist he may be but an expert in the occult he most certainly is not! Why the devil did you even ask him to join in the first place?'

'I'll admit that was a whim,' said Lord Ringmore. 'You see, I bumped into John the same day I acquired the book. He was visiting the club. It occurred to me he might be able to help.'

'And what about the escapologist?'

'You know as well as I that there is no one better qualified to cut through the dressings of deception, and Clay is currently doing his best to reclaim the book.' Lord Ringmore's voice grew louder as he grew agitated. 'He has aligned himself with a group of believers, yet *he* does not worry about his reputation.'

'I think you'll find his reputation is just about all Clay

cares about,' said Sir Tyrrell, very much enjoying seeing his phlegmatic friend so rattled.

Lord Ringmore banged his walking stick. 'Clay is out there, hunting this pair of thirteen-year-old orphans, because he knows they are the only thing that stands between us and the endless possibilities of the universe. What are you doing about it?'

Sir Tyrrell paused. He rubbed his chin and sat forward with renewed interest. 'Thirteen years old, you say?'

'Or thereabouts, yes,' said Lord Ringmore, dismissively. 'What does it matter?'

Sir Tyrrell smiled. In all the years he had known Lord Ringmore he had never seen him so agitated. 'Tell me, Silas, what's all this really about?'

'What do you mean?'

'I've had this nagging feeling there's something you haven't told us since that first meeting.'

'You know exactly what it's about,' said Lord Ringmore.

'Magic, yes,' Sir Tyrrell said. 'But what would you do with such unlimited power? There's a fair amount of power in this building but you've never shown any interest in that.'

Lord Ringmore stood up and walked to the window. He looked down at the river and spoke with his back to Sir Tyrrell. 'There is a spell,' he began. 'A spell for which Olwyn Broe spent her entire life searching. According to Mr Hayman, it is known as the Eternity Spell.'

'What does it do?'

Lord Ringmore turned back to face him. 'It is the spell

which can conquer death itself.'

'Immortality?' Sir Tyrrell sat back in his chair and considered Lord Ringmore's words. He pressed his hands together and rested his chin on the tips of his fingers. 'Interesting,' he said. 'Very interesting.'

'We are closer than we've ever been but the Society needs your help. Please, Augustus,' urged Lord Ringmore.

'I'll admit that for someone who rarely sets foot in the chamber you make a persuasive argument when necessary,' said Sir Tyrrell. 'But I'm sorry. I will not be forced into this decision. We will discuss it at a later stage. Now, if you don't mind I have work to get on with.'

27

Saved

Esther could see the fire on the other side of the river. It was the signal. Tom was telling her to get out. Perhaps he had learnt about Clay or maybe it was some other danger. Either way, she needed to distract Clay to make her getaway, but it was hopeless. He was watching her like a hawk.

'What's so special about this book anyway?' she asked, casually.

'You tell me. I didn't cover a man in flour to get it,' replied Clay.

'I just thought there might be some coin in it, you know, seeing as how keen Ringmore is on it.'

'You thought Ringmore would pay for a book you stole from him?'

Esther shrugged.

'You're probably right,' admitted Clay. 'He would have done.'

'So you don't believe what Ringmore says about it?' asked Esther.

'Ha! You do know more than you were letting on,' exclaimed Clay. 'No, I think this whole business is an impressive trick but, you see, there's very little I find more intriguing than a good trick. And what's especially interesting about this one is that I can't detect who's behind it. Imagine being shown a magic trick so neat that you don't even know who the magician is.'

'You don't think it's Lord Ringmore?'

'I don't think so. I've known him long enough to know when he believes something. If he is a salesman he's one who actually believes in the product he's selling.'

'Ow,' Esther cried, feeling claws dig into her leg. The black cat jumped off, ran to the door and started scratching at the wood.

'Your cat wants to go out,' said Clay.

'She's not my cat,' replied Esther.

Clay opened the door and smoke billowed into the room, filling Esther's lungs and making her cough. Behind the door, flames devoured the rotten insides of the building.

'Orphans? Oh, orphans! Can you hear me, orphans?' yelled Hardy from the other side of the fire. 'I'm teaching you a lesson. No one messes with me. Now, you're going to burn. You hear that, orphans? Burn.'

Esther could hear the rest of the gang laughing. The fire was growing in ferocity, crackling as it greedily ate away at the house's damp wooden beams. The cat sprang up onto the windowsill and disappeared out onto the ledge.

'We can't get out this way,' said Clay, backing away from the door.

'We'll have to go round,' said Esther. 'Follow me.'

Esther quickly climbed out of the window with Clay close behind her. She edged along the side of the building, pressing her fingertips against the wall. The metal railing on the outside of the building was icy cold, but Esther could feel the heat of the fire through the brickwork. She took another step and would have slipped had Clay not grabbed her arm.

'Take your time,' he said.

Esther took another couple of cautious steps but when she reached the edge of the building she saw that the wooden framework beneath them was on fire, making it impossible to reach the ground.

'There's no way here,' she said.

'Then we'll have to jump into the river,' said Clay.

'I can't!'

'We haven't much choice.'

'I can't swim,' she admitted.

'Esther,' said Clay. 'You have my guarantee that I will not let you drown. Take my hand and we'll jump together.'

Esther stared down at the cold river. Its murky waters lapped against the bankside as chunks of the burning building dropped into it. The water looked dark and dangerous. She turned to Clay. He nodded at her, apparently reading her mind again. She took his hand and felt its warmth as they tipped forward and jumped into the Thames.

Esther braced herself for the impact of icy water, but instead of a sudden, violent rush as she sunk beneath the surface, she landed on something as soft as a pillow. She felt Clay's hand tear away from hers as another, much stronger and bigger, took hold of her. Clay splashed down into the water, but Esther remained above it. She looked to see what she had landed on and realised that the River Thames had risen up in the shape of a giant hand, holding her on the surface tension of its palm.

She saw Clay resurface and look at her in astonishment. Then the huge watery hand moved, carrying Esther to the other side of the river, creating waves as it went. Inside the transparent hand were bits of debris from the river. The moonlight caught it and Esther saw a fish trapped inside its angled thumb. It was extraordinary. Unbelievable. She thought about all those stories the nuns used to tell them about God parting the water for Moses and wondered, could this be the hand of God, reaching out to protect her?

28

Collapse

Although the river spell had been a little rough around the edges, Mondriat had to admit it showed promise. Tom had not referred to the book at all, which was a good sign. Conjury was much better when it came from the Conjuror's own imagination. Conjury was supposed to be instinctive. It was a natural process. A true Conjuror looked into his heart, not into the pages of some book. But what use was that if the boy refused to listen to him? He needed to cast his True Reflection into a mirror that could not easily be smashed or discovered. Until then, performing any spell was highly dangerous, let alone such richly complex Conjury as the river spell. It was no surprise at all that Tom collapsed once Esther was safe, making the girl scream and run to his side.

'Tom!' she wailed. 'What's wrong, Tom?'

'I'll tell you what's wrong. Your foolish friend just performed extremely advanced Conjury while his spirit is still dangerously untethered,' explained Mondriat. 'I warned him. I did warn him.'

Esther looked at him. 'Evening, Mister Magpie,' she said.

'*Evening Mister Magpie*,' Mondriat squawked. 'This boy is half dead because of you and all you can say is Evening Mister Magpie. You need to take him somewhere safe so that he may recover.'

Esther turned back to look after Tom.

It was hopeless. Mondriat could talk until his beak fell off but his words were nothing but the meaningless prattle of a magpie to this unInfected girl.

Tom stirred, half opening his eyes. 'Esther,' he said vaguely.

'Happy now, Tom? Happy, are you?' exclaimed Mondriat. 'I told you this would happen. You didn't listen.'

'I had to save her.'

'Well, now she has to save you. Tell your friend to get you somewhere safe, somewhere you can recover properly.'

Tom looked at Esther. 'The crypt,' he said. 'Take me to the crypt.'

'All right.'

Mondriat watched as Esther helped him to his feet. Tom's loyalty to the girl was to his credit, but performing such bold Conjury in plain view was pure folly. The Conjurors of old did not demonstrate their powers with showy displays. Powerful Conjurors moved within the shadows. Tom had a great deal to learn. Mondriat only hoped the foolish child was around long enough to learn it.

And if he didn't recover? What then? Where would that leave Mondriat? Well, he thought. At least the girl was also of Conjuring age too. Maybe he could persuade her to perform the Creation Spell and take Tom's place. Yes, that's what he would do.

29

Fred

Harry Clay and Fred Limb had been friends since their orphanage days. Clay, with his ability to make money, had always supported Fred financially, whereas Fred had looked after Clay in every other way. Over the years Fred had acted as butler, personal guard, theatrical agent, nurse and best friend, depending on Clay's needs at the time. While the rest of the world might have found Harry Clay's antics unfathomable and inexplicable, there was very little he could do to surprise his old friend, even when he turned up in the middle of the night, with clothes that were both singed and soaking wet.

'Out of a fire, into a sewer?' Fred held the door open for his old friend.

'Something like that.' Harry stepped inside.

'I'll get a towel.'

'First, I need you to go and fetch Lord Ringmore.'

'At this hour?'

'At this hour,' replied Clay.

'Something's happened?'

'Something has most definitely happened.'

'Shouldn't we run you a bath and fetch you a brandy first? Your new show opens in a couple of nights and you don't want to catch a chill.'

'As soon as you go I promise I'll do both those things,' said Clay.

'I'll get my hat,' said Fred.

'Thank you, Fred.'

By the time Fred had returned with Lord Ringmore, Clay had bathed, wrapped himself in several layers of his warmest clothing and drunk enough brandy to warm a polar bear. He was sitting in front of a roaring fire nursing an empty brandy glass when Fred led Lord Ringmore into the room then left. Lord Ringmore noticed the posters and props that filled the walls.

'They're mementoes from my career,' explained Clay. 'Fred puts them up. I'm not one for wallowing in past glories but he's a sentimental old fool.'

'What's this one?' asked Lord Ringmore, indicating a rusty old chain that hung above the fireplace.

'The first chain from which I ever escaped,' replied Clay. 'Fred hung it there as a symbol of our own escape from destitution and poverty. Me, I'd have sold it for scrap.'

'So why have you summoned me? Have you got the book?' said Lord Ringmore, eagerly.

'Not yet,' said Clay, 'but, Silas, I have seen what it can

do. I witnessed the Thames itself rise up and save the girl from drowning. I watched an enormous hand carry her across the river. It was the single most extraordinary sight I have ever seen. You were right, Ringmore. You were right all along. Magic. It exists. Real magic.'

'You saw it? You witnessed real magic?' gasped Lord Ringmore.

'With these eyes.'

'So where is the book? Who is using its powers?'

'I believe it is the orphans themselves.'

'Then we must waste no time in finding them,' said Lord Ringmore.

'Silas, I need a moment to take all this in,' said Clay. 'Magic. Can you imagine what I could do with such powers?'

'This isn't something to be squandered on a stage, Clay.'

'Yes, but everything I believed, everything I thought I knew, it was all wrong. My world has been turned upside down.'

'You were a closed-minded cynic and now your eyes have been prized open,' exclaimed Lord Ringmore angrily. 'Whereas I, Harry, I have always known there was something else. So try to imagine how I feel as I hear that you allowed it to slip through your fingers this evening.'

'Calm down,' said Clay. 'We'll get the book, it's just a matter of time. But don't you want to know how these orphans unlocked its mysteries when we could not?'

'It *is* perplexing,' he agreed. 'I will gather the other members. Now, tell me what you saw. Spare no detail. I want to hear it all.'

30

Crypt

The crypt beneath the church in Shadwell was another of the orphans' hide-spots. Tom had never been overly keen on it. He said it made him feel like a trapped animal, but Esther believed his objection had more to do with the spookiness of the damp, dark underground room.

Esther half dragged, half guided the semi-conscious Tom away from the river, across the churchyard and down the stone steps into the crypt, closely followed by the hopping magpie. When she lay Tom down, she took the book from his left hand but was unable to prize the thick branch from his right.

It was a cold night and she was tired, so Esther lay down with her arms around Tom for warmth. Tom made no movement at all now, but at least his breathing seemed even and deep. Eventually Esther fell into a restless, shivering sleep in spite of the questions that buzzed around her mind. When she awoke from an intangible nightmare, she sat up to find Tom with his arms wrapped around his legs, gently rocking.

'Tom?' she said. 'What's happened to you?'

'Where's Mondriat?' he said, ignoring the question.

'Who?'

'The magpie. Where did he go?'

'You mean that disgusting bird? It flew off after we arrived.'

'He was right. I need to find a mirror,' said Tom. 'I can feel this stuff eating my insides.'

'What stuff? I don't understand.'

'I performed the Creation Spell and became Infected. Now the lifeblood wants to return to its source.'

Esther didn't understand what he was saying but she was certain of one thing; as incredible as it seemed, the hand that had rescued her had belonged to Tom.

Tom picked up the book and handed it to her. 'You were right about this, Esther. It's a book of spells. I used it to perform my first one; but the river, that was my own Conjury,' replied Tom. 'I did it myself.'

'It was wonderful, Tom. It was like nothing I've ever seen, but how . . .'

'I can show you how.' Tom's eyes widened. 'I'll show you how you can become like me. You can perform the Creation Spell then you'll see things as I see them.' As he spoke, it was as though his words filled him with renewed energy. 'You see things better. I can't explain how strong I feel. I raised the water but if I'd wanted I could have done the same to every living thing in this stinking city.'

'Tom, you're scaring me,' said Esther.

'You don't need to be scared no more.' He took her hand in his. 'You're cold,' he said. He moved his staff on the ground and Esther felt warmth spread from his fingers and fill her body.

He released her hand and she saw a wart rise up from the skin on his arm.

'What is that?' asked Esther.

'It's the lifeblood. It happens every time I perform a spell. Don't worry, Mondriat says it'll go down once I've done the Mirror Spell.'

'Mondriat the magpie?'

'He was a Conjuror once,' said Tom. 'And he's right. I need to find a mirror. Then I'll be able to do whatever I want.'

It was early morning when Esther and Tom left the crypt and jumped onto the back of a bus that took them as far as Ludgate Circus, where swarms of smartly dressed businessmen were making a show of looking important and busy.

'We need to be careful. We ain't so far from Hardy's patch here,' said Esther.

'I ain't scared of Hardy no more,' said Tom. 'My eyes are open now. These toffs who think they know it all, they haven't a clue about anything.' With a swirl of his staff and a wave of his hand he sent a gust of wind that caught several gentlemen by surprise and sent their top hats tumbling down the road. Tom laughed as they ran after them. 'We've been on the bottom of the rung all this time; but not for much longer! Come on now, I'll fetch us some breakfast.'

'We can use the money we made from Ringmore's robbery,' said Esther.

'Not today.'

'But I see no opportunities for thieving round here,' she said. 'We should head Aldwych way.'

'No. Today we'll eat a cooked breakfast. Stay here.' Tom crossed the busy road. For a moment, Esther lost him behind a passing coach. When he reappeared he was standing on the opposite side of the pavement in front of a fancy restaurant. It was the kind of city establishment with prices as inflated as its customers' bellies. A doorman in a gold-buttoned uniform stood outside, welcoming in those who could afford to eat there and turning away those who looked as if they could not.

Seeing Tom approach, he looked as impassable as a brick wall but Tom stopped in front of him and scratched his staff on the ground. On the other side of the road, Esther couldn't hear what he said but, to her surprise, the doorman instantly stood to one side and allowed Tom into the restaurant.

Esther scrambled up onto the window ledge of the bank she'd been standing outside to see what was happening inside the restaurant, but a weedy-voiced bank clerk quickly emerged and ordered her down. When Tom reappeared he was carrying a tray with two plates stacked high with food. He thanked the doorman politely and made his way across the road.

'What did you do?' asked Esther, when he reached her.

'I can make them do anything I want,' said Tom. 'Anything.'

'It doesn't seem to last that long by the looks of things though,' said Esther.

In front of the restaurant a commotion was brewing as an angry-looking maître d' came out, hauling a waiter by the collar and addressing the doorman. The doorman pointed to Tom.

'Let's go,' said Esther.

'Why?' said Tom. 'I'll just do the same to him.'

'No,' said Esther. 'It's not good for you. Besides, we can't keep drawing attention to ourselves. It ain't just Hardy. Ringmore wants his book back too.'

'What does it matter? I can make us disappear.' He smirked then added, with a glint in his eye, 'Or I can make them disappear.'

'Please,' said Esther. 'Let's just go.'

The maître d' was now dragging the waiter and the doorman across the busy road. Tom followed Esther. In spite of the angry man's cries of 'Stop thief!' it didn't take the orphans long to lose their pursuers. They knew these streets and alleyways as well as anyone.

31

Democracy

John Symmonds was beginning to have doubts about the Society of Thirteen. While the other members already had a fascination for supernaturalism, he had never expressed any such interest. Increasingly, he was coming to the conclusion that his time was being wasted. He had decided that the lines and shapes which filled the pages of the book were no language. If they were a code, it was one which was only intelligible to the creator.

Nor did Mr Symmonds appreciate being dragged south of the river to such a grim spot at such an early hour. A meeting held in a gentlemen's club was one thing, but the burnt-out shell of a Rotherhithe warehouse was hardly a civilised place to gather. The idea of asking Kiyaya to stay outside was a little preposterous too, since there was very little distinction between the interior and the exterior of the building but, as usual, Lord Ringmore was insistent, so Kiyaya stood on the other side of the non-existent door.

'Much has happened since our last meeting and it is my duty to inform you that at present the book is not in our possession,' said Lord Ringmore.

'Not in our possession?' echoed Mr Symmonds.

'It was stolen from Ringmore's house during our last meeting,' said Clay.

'Then why are we here?' Mr Symmonds demanded.

'This place was home to the orphans who now have the book,' said Clay, 'until it was set alight last night by a local gang. I've been searching for clues but, so far, nothing.'

'All this for an incomprehensible book,' said Mr Symmonds, with a heavy sigh.

'Not incomprehensible to everyone, it would seem,' said Clay.

'What do you mean?' demanded Mr Symmonds. 'It's unreadable.'

'I have seen what it can do,' said Clay. 'I have witnessed its power. I have seen magic, gentlemen. Real magic. The waters of the Thames itself rose up in the form of a giant hand.'

'Is this true? The orphans have awoken its power?' said Mr G. Hayman.

'Thirteen-year-old orphans,' said Sir Tyrrell, looking at her meaningfully.

'Your investigations have revealed something?' said Lord Ringmore.

'Not a complete picture,' said Mr G. Hayman, 'but from what Sir Tyrrell and I were told by one of my interviewees it seems that your orphan messengers were ideally placed to realise the book's potential.'

'Then it is imperative that we reclaim both it and them, using every resource available to us.' Lord Ringmore turned to Sir Tyrrell.

'Ah, this again?' said Sir Tyrrell.

'Now is the time,' said Lord Ringmore. 'If we are to reclaim our book and quickly, we will need more help looking for these two thieving urchins. We need the police to find them.'

Sir Tyrrell coughed, but grumpily waved Mr G. Hayman away when she tried to pat him on the back. 'I will not risk my parliamentary position by abusing my powers for this –'

'It is not an abuse,' said Lord Ringmore. 'What could be more important than the knowledge we seek?'

'For goodness' sake. We're talking about a pair of orphans,' said Sir Tyrrell. 'Do you not think this an overreaction?'

'*I* do not,' said Lord Ringmore. 'But what have the other members to say? After all, I see no reason why the Society of Thirteen shouldn't operate according to democratic principles.'

'If you ask me,' said Clay, 'this situation is far too delicate for the brutes in the police force. I'm with Sir Tyrrell.'

'I am grateful for your support if not for your reasoning,' said Sir Tyrrell.

Lord Ringmore's annoyance was evident in the scowl on his face. 'Sir Tyrrell and Mr Clay have made their opinions known,' he said. 'I vote in favour of employing the eyes of the police to reclaim the book, which makes it two to one. So the decision lies with the remaining two Society members.'

'I suppose Lord Ringmore's case makes sense,' said Mr Symmonds, although he sounded as if he really wasn't fussed either way. 'If we are to get the book we may as well use the police.'

'Two all, meaning the deciding vote lies with Mr Hayman,' said Lord Ringmore.

'But . . . But . . .' blustered Sir Tyrrell.

'But what?' Mr G. Hayman asked innocently. She looked at Sir Tyrrell, her eyes daring him to say what was on his mind: that she was a woman; what right had she to vote? Sir Tyrrell said nothing. Mr G. Hayman smiled then said, 'We are close to our goal, but we need the book and we need the orphans. This is all that matters now. I vote in favour of Ringmore's plan.'

'That's three against two,' said Lord Ringmore, clapping his hands triumphantly.

Sir Tyrrell exhaled in exasperation but conceded his loss with a non-verbal exclamation.

'I will speak to the Chief Commissioner about a special operation,' conceded Sir Tyrrell. 'But what am I to tell him?'

'I will leave that up to your imagination,' said Lord Ringmore.

'I wonder, do politicians have imaginations?' enquired Mr G. Hayman.

'I assure you,' replied Sir Tyrrell, 'that when it comes to the creation of believable yet fallacious stories, a politician is far more adept than any novelist.'

32

Rainfall

Even the potent mixture of dubious smells in the alleyway could not detract from the delicious tastes that exploded in Esther's mouth as she devoured the last few morsels of the stolen breakfast and licked the plate clean.

'From now on we'll breakfast like this every day,' said Tom. 'Whenever we want, as much as we want.' He raised his hand and made the empty plates hover, spinning round and round.

'It's unbelievable, Tom,' admitted Esther, gazing at them. 'All of it.'

'This is just the start,' he replied. 'With power like this we'll soon have Hardy answering to us.' His eyes sparkled with wild magic.

'With power like this you should forget him and leave this life behind,' said Esther.

'He tried to kill you,' said Tom. 'He set fire to our home. For that, he'll pay.'

Tom winced as another wart appeared on a finger. He closed his hand into a fist and the plates dropped and smashed on the ground.

'Don't look at me like that,' he snapped. 'It'll be fine. I'll find a mirror like Mondriat said and the warts will go down.'

'You trust this magpie then?'

'Everything he said has been true so far.'

'What does he want? Why can't I understand him?'

'You will be able to understand him when you do the Creation Spell.'

'I don't know, Tom,' said Esther, hesitantly.

'You need to see the world as I do, Est. It's amazing. You feel . . . you feel like a god.'

'Gods don't faint . . . or get warts for that matter.'

'Look, I can't make you do it. But you've got the book. You see that shape on the back? Find a stick and draw it on the ground then step into the middle. Here, you could use this.' He picked up a discarded broom handle that had been leaning against the side of a wall and handed it to Esther.

She looked at it uncertainly. 'It's just so much to take in. Remember what Mother Agnes used to say about selling your soul. Nothing comes for free.'

After agreeing to meet later that day at one of their hide-spots in Spitalfields, Tom left Esther and went in search of a mirror. Alone in the alleyway, Esther thought about a day at the orphanage when she had asked Mother Agnes why miracles didn't happen any more like they used to in Bible days. Before the inevitable beating for asking insolent questions, Mother Agnes explained that the events in the testaments occurred during a time when heaven was closer to earth. 'More extraordinary things were possible back then,' she had said. Watching Tom walk away, Esther wondered whether everything they had been taught was wrong.

She turned the book over in her hands and thought that perhaps things would have been better if she had never suggested they work that square in Piccadilly. They would never have met Lord Ringmore and none of this would have happened. She ran her fingers over the number on the front. She opened it to the last page and marvelled at the complex pattern that filled the paper. She closed it and looked at the shape on the back cover. A circle within a triangle within a circle. The Creation Spell. It was such a simple shape. Could it really draw such power from the earth? There was so much she did not understand.

She opened the book again and flicked through the pages. The more she stared the more they spoke to her. It was wordless speech, heavy with meaning. She tried to close the book but it would not shut. Something was happening to her. The world swam. She only closed her eyes for a moment but when she opened them she saw, on the ground, scratched into the dust, three shapes. A circle within a triangle within a circle. They had been drawn by the broom handle she was holding, but she had no memory of doing so. It was as though a sleeping corner of her mind had awoken and formed the shapes. She could feel it urging her forward. It was too strong to resist. Esther stepped into the centre of the shape and felt raw energy rush through her body.

A droplet of water splashed on her face and she looked up to see a cloud bursting. The falling rain was strange and slow. Esther saw every droplet in such detail that she saw London reflected a thousand times over. It fell so slowly that Esther had time to step under the cover of an overhanging roof before the shower came down. She watched the unutterable beauty of the rain hitting the paving stones and washing away the shapes she had drawn.

Tom was right. It felt amazing.

33

Voice

Whether or not it was the voice downstairs that awoke John Symmonds at such an ungodly hour was unclear but, now that he was awake, he felt compelled to go and investigate. Reaching his bedroom door, it occurred to him that it could be a house breaker so he took the precaution of arming himself with an iron fire poker before continuing down the stairs. He was halfway down when he realised three curious things about the voice. Firstly, its deep, resonant tones were undoubtedly those of his manservant, Kiyaya. Secondly, remarkably, Kiyaya was speaking English. Thirdly, the conversation in which he was engaged was notably one-sided.

John Symmonds stepped carefully to avoid the squeaky floorboards as he reached the hallway at the bottom of the stairs.

'What interest have you in this matter?' said Kiyaya, demonstrating first-rate pronunciation and the admirable use of an intransitive verb.

To Mr Symmonds' even greater surprise the reply came not in the form of a second voice but as the unmistakable meow of a cat. Even more curiously, Kiyaya appeared to have no trouble understanding its meaning.

'If I were to help you, what could you do for me?' he replied, revealing the ability to use a conditional clause correctly.

John Symmonds was taken aback. When he had met Kiyaya, the American Indian had been living as a hermit, cast out by his tribe. He had never seen a white man before, nor heard of a land across the ocean called England. He had seemed to Mr Symmonds a good man with a gentle soul, so why this deceit? Why had he hidden his ability to not just understand but speak English? Then it struck him. Of course. Kiyaya was sleepwalking. Mr Symmonds had recently read of another similar case, a man who, in his waking hours could only speak English, but who spoke perfect Italian in his sleep. That was it. Kiyaya had picked up the linguistic patterns of English in his unconscious mind. The possibility of this phenomenon was intriguing. How fascinating were the depths of the human mind!

The meowing, however, remained a mystery. Intrigued to learn more, Mr Symmonds opened the door and found Kiyaya addressing a black cat perched on a table. They both turned to look at him. Neither cat nor man spoke, but John Symmonds became overly aware that he must have looked distinctly odd himself, dressed in a nightgown and clutching a poker. He lowered the weapon. Kiyaya didn't look asleep.

'What an intriguing fellow you are, Kiyaya,' Mr Symmonds said. 'You pick up our language but, instead of telling me, you reveal it to this cat. I should explain that in our culture, the only people who engage in conversations with members of the animal kingdom reside within the confines of Bedlam.'

'John Symmonds,' said Kiyaya. 'I am grateful for all you have done for me. You brought me to this land, so I am sorry it must end like this.'

'End? End like what?' asked Mr Symmonds.

The Indian moved his staff across the floor and placed a heavy hand on Mr Symmonds' shoulder. Seconds later, John Symmonds collapsed to the floor. Dead.

34

Longdale

Hardy and his boys were heading down New Oxford Street when a small army of coppers appeared out of nowhere. Hardy turned to flee but saw yet more coming the other way. They were surrounded. Brewer reached for his knife, but Hardy shook his head. They wouldn't be fighting their way out of this one. The policemen formed a circle around them, holding truncheons in their hands but saying nothing. If one of the shopkeepers had talked, thought Hardy, revenge would be both swift and bloody.

A smartly dressed gentleman wearing round spectacles pushed through the ranks. In spite of his brown chequered suit, his manner gave him away as a copper.

'How can I help you today, officer?' asked Hardy.

'My name is Chief Inspector Longdale,' said the man.

'That supposed to impress us?' said Brewer.

'I'm not here to impress you, Brewer,' he replied.

Upon hearing his name, Brewer glanced nervously at the

others, but Hardy was maintaining eye contact with the Chief Inspector.

'Office copper walking the beat, getting his hands dirty for a change, eh?' said Hardy.

Longdale smiled at him, then, without warning, punched him hard in the stomach. Hardy doubled over in pain, winded by the unexpected attack. Stump and Worms stepped forward but the surrounding officers raised their truncheons threateningly.

Longdale grabbed the back of Hardy's coat and lifted his head so that he could whisper into his ear. 'I may be a desk copper but I've got hands plenty dirty enough to deal with you.'

'What's all this about?' gasped Hardy.

Longdale placed an arm over his shoulder and led him through the ranks of men, away from the others.

'Ne'er-do-wells like you think you're as invisible as the rats in the sewers,' said Longdale. 'I'm here to remind you that you are not. As you can see, my men outnumber your boys and we can bring you in and have you swing whenever we choose.'

'On what charge?' demanded Hardy.

'Charges are easy enough to find, especially for street vermin like you,' said Longdale. 'You get on the wrong side of me and that punch will feel like a tickle.'

'Kind of felt like that anyway,' said Hardy.

Longdale brought his face up close to Hardy's. 'Do you think this is a joke, lad? You won't be laughing once you're standing up on a scaffold.'

'So you've come to threaten me, is that it?' said Hardy.

'No,' replied Longdale. 'I've come to help you. Most people would look at you and see a lost cause. Me? I see a lost soul and it is my Christian duty to find lost souls and to help save them.'

'You've come to Holborn looking for repentance, have you copper?' said Hardy. 'I think you're in the wrong job.'

'There was a fire down in Rotherhithe,' said Longdale. 'Nasty business. A warehouse went up. The fire even spread to the neighbouring properties. A lot of damage caused. Not the first time either. A lot of the shops you frequent seem to end up in cinders, don't they?'

'So?'

'You know how long you can go down for arson, Hardy?'

He said nothing.

'Thankfully no one was hurt,' said Longdale.

'No one?' replied Hardy.

'I thought that might surprise you. Although witnesses did see a gang of four lads leaving the scene.'

'Listen, if you'd wanted to arrest me you'd have done so,' said Hardy. 'You must want something else. You want me to turn blower? Is that it? You want me to turn someone in?'

'The occupants of this warehouse,' said Longdale. 'We believe they were a pair of orphans, like yourself. In fact, we believe they came from the same institution you did. They survived this fire.'

'Did they?' snarled Hardy.

'I'd like a word with them.'

'Why?'

Longdale shook his head. 'I'm the one looking for answers here. I'm charged with finding these orphans. I'm to use every tool at my disposal. Every tool, Hardy.'

'You got a city full of coppers and you want my help?' said Hardy.

'In my experience, rats are hard to hunt because they scurry off at first sight and take cover in their grubby little rat-holes. The best way to find a rat is to send in another after it.'

'What happens if I find them?' asked Hardy.

'Bring them in and maybe we'll delay that walk to the scaffold,' replied Longdale.

35

Olwyn

Mondriat was following Tom's progress through the streets. Finally the foolish boy had ditched the girl and gone in search of his mirror, and Mondriat wanted to be there when he chose it. A pigeon landed on the roof in front of him, blocking his view, so he sent it away with a sharp peck. Mondriat hated pigeons. The scavenging vermin of London were stupid animals, but they did have an innate ability to identify a bird with purpose. Assuming he had spotted food, more of them flocked around him on the edge of the building. Mondriat flapped his wings aggressively to keep them back but was surprised when the entire flock took to the sky. He turned around and saw the reason. A black cat prowled towards him, its green eyes focused on him. The same cat he had seen several times before.

'It would be better for you if you didn't,' warned Mondriat.

If the cat sunk its teeth into his body Mondriat would tear his spirit from the bird's body and enter the cat's. He would push aside its weak, feline spirit and take control of its legs, eyes and teeth. He would become the cat. He had done it before but he currently had no desire to be a cat nor to taste the decomposed magpie's body he currently wore.

He had extended his wings and was about to leave when the cat spoke. 'Hello, Mondriat.'

'Olwyn?' he replied.

'It's been a long time,' said the cat.

'I thought you dead.'

'And I thought you harmless,' whispered Olwyn. 'It seems we were both mistaken.'

'What harm am I doing?' asked Mondriat.

'You are following the boy to learn which mirror he chooses.'

'There's no harm in knowing, is there?'

'What are you up to, Mondriat?' asked the cat.

'You know me.' Mondriat flapped his wings casually. 'I'm just following the flow of the river.'

'I don't believe you. You haven't changed.'

'That's where you are wrong,' protested Mondriat. 'I have had a long time to think about what I did. I thought that I could take others' Conjury and make myself stronger but I couldn't cheat death. I couldn't stop the decay. In the end, neither of us could.'

The cat stepped on a loose tile, sending it sliding forward. Mondriat flew up and avoided it. It slipped on the edge and crashed to the ground.

'This form suits you,' said Mondriat, landing back on the roof.

'As the body of a thieving magpie suits you,' replied Olwyn.

'I told you, I have changed. A century of eating raw birds' eggs will do that to a man. We failed, Olwyn. We both sought the Eternity Spell and we both failed, so we settled for this inferior animal existence,' said Mondriat.

'Your efforts eradicated Conjury from this land. Mine did not.'

'Yes, well, you know, I wanted a way for both of us to live on, but you were always one step ahead of me. Such a clever Conjuress, always playing such elaborate games. I did it all for you.'

'I never asked you to kill in my name.'

'The book's yours, isn't it?' said Mondriat. 'I recognised your style as soon as I saw the ripples of that protection spell. Beautiful Conjury, Olwyn. You always did cast the most exquisite spells. But what is it for? Why did you write it?'

'The book is not important.'

Mondriat stared hard at the black cat, trying to see a glimpse of Olwyn's expressions. She had never displayed a great deal of facial expression as a human, and as a cat she was utterly unreadable.

'You have the boy now, but you will leave the girl alone,' she said.

'Why? What's so special about her? What's this all about?'

'I know better than to trust you,' said Olwyn. 'I'm simply telling you to stay away.'

'Can't you let me in, Olwyn? Can't we work together

again? I do miss you.'

'Betrayal is in your nature,' said Olwyn. 'You are still the same man you always were. Instinctive, passionate, dangerous . . .'

Mondriat smiled inwardly. 'The very reasons you married me,' he said.

'That was a very long time ago,' replied Olwyn, turning and making her way across the rooftops, her tail raised high.

36

Reflection

The Mirror Spell itself was simple enough, comprising of three circles, a triangle and four connecting lines. The tricky thing was to find an appropriate mirror. Mondriat had told Tom it needed to be accessible, so there was no point choosing one inside a restaurant or a barber's shop as he needed to perform the spell without arousing suspicion. A pub on Drury Lane boasted a large one on the back wall with swirly writing on the surface. It was a good size, but fights often broke out in pubs and there was a danger it might get smashed. 'Picking a safe mirror is vital,' Mondriat had said, 'but you must also keep your mirror secret. Many Conjurors lost their lives after their True Reflections were drawn out and their Conjury was stolen.'

Approaching Hardy's patch, Tom's pace slowed. No more spells, he had promised Esther, but if Hardy came after him what choice would he have? On the corner of Bloomsbury Street he noticed a shop that sold umbrellas and walking sticks with its name printed proudly above the display window: James Smith & Sons. Tom had hung around outside this shop before, waiting to pickpocket its wealthy customers, but he had never really thought about the items it sold before. A black stick with a gold handle like Lord Ringmore's was on display in the window. Tom looked down at the rough stick in his hand, sensing its inadequacy. He wondered whether the man inside would be able to polish and lacquer it and turn it into a finer looking thing. It was his staff and it deserved to look as powerful and magnificent as a toff's walking stick. Then he noticed the mirror on the side of a pillar behind the stick. Protected by the glass of the shop window and yet visible from the street, it was perfect.

To anyone passing, Tom looked like a boy playing idly with a stick as he drew the spell. Tom fixed his eyes on his own reflection. The city sounds ebbed away as Tom completed the spell and raised his left hand towards the mirror. A thick mist spread across its surface. His reflection vanished from sight. Tom felt panicked, fearing something had gone wrong, then his reflection stepped through the mist and smiled at him. 'Hello, Tom,' he heard his own voice say.

Tom stared at his reflection, dumbfounded.

His reflection laughed.

Tom didn't like being laughed at, not even by himself. 'What's so funny?' he demanded.

'Look at you, Tom,' said his reflection. 'You have the power to do anything now. You need never be hungry again, you can bend and shape this world to do what you want.

So what's stopping you get what you really want?'

Tom looked at the image of his own face and saw more faces. Shadows of those who made him. He saw with renewed clarity how he was the product of a mother and a father, unknown to him yet present in every feature. They were there in the colour of his eyes, the shape of his mouth and the texture of his hair. He could not escape who he was or where he came from. Finally he understood what the question meant. Finally he could see the answer.

'Family,' he whispered. 'I want my family.'

His reflection nodded.

'I told you to clear off,' said a voice.

The mist had gone. Tom was in front of the shop again. A shop assistant had stepped out of the door and was addressing him angrily. 'I've been banging on that window telling you as much for long enough. This is not Madam Tussaud's. Now clear off.'

'No need for that, mate,' said Tom. 'After all, I'm a customer.'

Tom moved his staff on the ground and confidently raised his left hand.

37

Changing

Lord Ringmore could find no suitable place to sit in Clay's untidy bed chamber so he remained standing. 'It seems John's body was found by the maid he employed to clean the house,' he said. 'The poor woman ran out into the road, screaming hysterically until neighbours came to see what the fuss was about.'

Clay, who was changing behind a screen, poked his head around the side. 'It's a terrible business. What did you say was the cause of death?'

'The attending physician believes his heart gave up on him but the police coroner is yet to give his verdict.'

Clay's head disappeared again. 'Just goes to show, doesn't it? He seemed as right as rain the last time we saw him.'

'It is indeed a brutal reminder of the fragility of life,' agreed Lord Ringmore. 'We are but fleeting shadows, living on borrowed time.'

'What will happen to John's native now?'

'That's another odd thing about the business. When the maid arrived she said the house was empty. Kiyaya had gone.'

'Was anything missing? Could it have been some kind of robbery?'

'Nothing was taken and, unless Kiyaya has the ability to stop a man's heart, there is no reason to suspect foul play. Still, I gather the police would like to speak to him, providing they can find him and someone who can translate for them.'

'It would hardly be difficult to find a man like that,' said Clay. 'A man the size of a small mountain, dressed in animal skins; even the old bill should be able to round him up.'

'That's true,' admitted Lord Ringmore. 'What on earth are you doing behind there, Harry?'

Clay stepped out from behind the screen. He was dressed in a ragged brown dress, stained, tattered and bunched up at the back, giving the appearance of a hunchback. He pulled a hat over his face and adopted a strange, limping walk, performing a perfect impersonation of one of London's many old begging women.

'Very impressive,' admitted Lord Ringmore. 'But what makes you think you will succeed in locating the orphans where the police have failed?'

'The police couldn't find a drink in a gin house,' said Clay. 'Talking of which . . .' He picked up a half-empty glass from the sideboard and downed its contents then shouted, 'Fred, come in here, will you?'

Fred entered the room.

‘Fill me up, will you, Fred?’ said Clay.

‘The potent stench of gin on your breath is all part of the act, is it?’ asked Fred.

‘Sometimes it’s hard to distinguish business from pleasure,’ replied Clay, grinning.

Fred took the empty glass from Clay’s hand and left the room.

‘You’re lucky to have a man like that,’ said Lord Ringmore. ‘Trustworthy servants are hard to come by.’

‘Me and Fred go way back,’ said Clay.

‘You haven’t told him about any of this though, I hope.’

‘I trust Fred more than anyone in the world but no, I haven’t told him and he knows not to ask.’

‘Perhaps I should accompany you today,’ said Lord Ringmore, anxiously.

‘No. You go researching with Hayman,’ said Clay. ‘Leave the book to me.’

‘The book is one aspect of our quest,’ said Lord Ringmore. ‘But if the orphans have awoken its potential then we need them as much as the book.’

‘When I get the book, the orphans will follow. You’ll see,’ replied Clay.

‘And you’ll tell me as soon as you have it,’ said Lord Ringmore.

‘Of course,’ replied Clay.

‘It is important that we work together on this.’

‘I won’t let you down,’ said Clay.

‘I hope not, Harry.’

Fred returned with the refilled glass. ‘Your gin,’ he said.

Clay took it but instead of drinking it, he threw it over himself, drenching his ragged attire.

'Now, if you don't mind I'd better get to work,' he said.

38

Mudstorm

Esther didn't know what to do with herself. The world was so much bigger, stranger and scarier than she could have imagined. She knew she should go to Spitalfields and wait for Tom but she needed to be alone. She needed to think. Still clutching the book, she felt herself drawn to the river, and soon found herself on the embankment. She felt the power of the river's flowing water. She drew comfort from its energy. The tide was out. The Earthsoul was exhaling. She followed stone steps down to a beach of mud and stone. She sat down on a rock and leaned her staff against her leg. She needed time to adjust to this. She opened the book and studied the diagrams that filled its pages. They made perfect sense to her now. She gazed at them, filled with wonder and awe. Conjury was beautiful.

An old woman with ragged clothes and a hunched back was making her way across the mud, searching through it for any treasure the Thames might have left behind. Even from such a distance, Esther could smell the gin on her breath. They must have looked like a pair of wretched souls down in the mud but Esther understood that they were both so much closer to the source of real power than any of the top-hatted businessmen of the city.

Esther felt exhausted by her racing thoughts but was unable to stop the questions that sprang into her mind. What should she do with such power? Was it her responsibility to wield it for her own good or the good of others? What had the Conjurors of old done? Where would all this end?

She didn't know how long she sat there but when she looked up she saw water lapping at her feet. The tide was coming in. Esther stood up to leave and saw Hardy and the gang descending the stone steps.

'Nice day for a stroll on the beach.' Hardy jumped down into the mud, not caring how it splattered his trousers.

'Leave me alone.' Esther placed the book on the rock behind her and picked up the broom handle.

'What you going to do with that?' Hardy asked, mockingly.

'I don't want to hurt you, Hardy,' said Esther.

'*You don't want to hurt me*?' he echoed. 'Even after I burnt down your home? You must be some kind of saint not to hold something like that against me. Is that right, Esther? You like one of them saints Mother Agnes used to bang on about?'

'No.'

'We've got a lot in common, you and me.'

‘I’m nothing like you.’

‘We both got our heads screwed on right. Not like that lot.’ Hardy gesticulated to the others, who watched from the steps. ‘Worms and Stump haven’t got a brain between them and Brewer, well, he’s way too fond of that knife. I need to keep him in his place more often than I’d like. You, though. You understand how things work.’

Hardy continued to approach, squelching through the thick mud.

‘You’re a pretty girl . . . under all that anger, I mean. I think it’s important for girls to be pretty. Fellas, well, they can be ugly as sin and do all right, but girls like you, a pretty face is gonna make all the difference.’ He was close enough to see the book on the rock behind her. ‘I keep wondering what all this is about,’ he said. ‘I reckon it’s got to be something to do with that book. Is that why all them coppers are looking for you?’

‘What are you talking about?’

‘Just what I said,’ he replied. ‘Now, why do you think they want you?’

‘I don’t know.’

‘Lucky it was me what found you first, eh? If you could only learn to trust me I’d be able to help you. I can keep you safe.’ He reached out to touch her hair, but Esther batted his hand away with the broom handle.

‘I can look after myself,’ she said.

Hardy laughed. He looked down at his muddy trousers. ‘It’s disgusting down here.’

‘No one asked you to come here.’

'You know I'd go anywhere for you,' said Hardy. 'Now, what about that kiss?'

He moved in but Esther pushed him, catching him off guard and sending him staggering back. He tripped on a rock and landed in the mud.

'Oi,' he shouted, alerting Brewer, Stump and Worms. They hurriedly rushed down the steps to help him.

'You shouldn't have done that,' said Hardy. He stood and tried to shake the mud from his hands.

'I won't tell you again,' said Esther.

'You won't have to.'

Hardy lurched forward but in a sudden flurry of movement, Esther spun around, making shapes on the ground with the broom handle, drawing power from the rich, oozing mud. With a wave of her left hand she sent a wall of mud up between them. Another movement and she whisked it into a spinning tornado. Hardy stared in disbelief as the mud swirled towards him. It lifted him off the ground, his arms and legs flailing. Stump, Worms and Brewer tried to get away but Esther sent the tornado at them. Her anger too easily turned to destructive power. She scooped them up and, with a final dramatic finish, lowered her hand and sent all four of them flying. They landed face down on the mud and the rocks.

Esther laughed as she watched them scrabble to their feet and run, but the power drained from her as the mud rained down and she felt weak. She went to pick up the book and saw that it was no longer on the rock behind her. The old lady had gone too. She turned to look for her but felt a sudden burst of pain as a wart pushed itself to the surface of the skin on her hand. She stared at it in horror, wondering, what had she done? What had she done?

39

Outcast

Judging by the astonished stares of its inhabitants, the East-End slum was not used to such well-to-do visitors as Mr G. Hayman and Lord Ringmore. Many would have felt decidedly uncomfortable under such scrutiny but this was not Mr G. Hayman's first visit and Lord Ringmore had encountered similar behaviour countless times during his travels around the world. He considered how the journey across town had taken less than an hour and yet they were surrounded by the kind of destitution one might expect from an African shanty town or the backwaters of India. One really could travel the world without ever leaving London.

The housing was every bit as pitiful as its occupants and many dwellings looked on the brink of collapse, giving Lord Ringmore cause to think twice before following Mr G. Hayman into one such ramshackle hut, with sloping walls and boarded-up windows. Inside, he was introduced to Mrs

Smith, an old woman with skin as dark and lined as the wooden beams that held up her decrepit dwelling. She sat huddled in a gloomy room, wrapped in blankets, in front of a fire that poured out more smoke than warmth. When Mr G. Hayman made the introduction, Mrs Smith let out a throaty laugh. 'A Lord. Well, Lord. Me honoured, my Lord.' She bowed her head and laughed some more.

Mr G. Hayman waited until she had finished. 'Lord Ringmore shares the same interest as me.'

Mrs Smith kissed her teeth and fixed her sharp eyes on him. 'You want to know about the old ways, huh? You care for the shadows? You a Lord of darkness?'

'I have spent my life in search of something beyond our understanding,' said Lord Ringmore.

'Something more? Look like you got everything you need, to me. I bet you never felt the pangs of hunger, Lord. But you came to me because you still hungry? That it, Lord?'

'Mrs Smith,' said Mr G. Hayman. 'The last time we spoke you told me of a man you met back in our home country, a man with powers.'

'That's right,' said Mrs Smith. 'A man who could melt mountains, drink rivers or move as the air. But power's no use if you outcast. Power's no good if you shunned.'

'Shunned by whom?' asked Lord Ringmore.

'This man tell me how they all outcast. They feared. And no wonder, given what men like him are capable of.'

'Mrs Smith spent several nights in the desert with this man,' said Mr G. Hayman.

'He like having someone to talk to,' the old woman added.

'What did he look like?' asked Lord Ringmore.

'His body was painted. Strange patterns on his skin and his eyes were like the blackest night I ever see. There was plenty of death in those eyes.'

'Please tell us,' said Mr G. Hayman. 'Did he ever mention something called the Eternity Spell?'

The old woman tutted reproachfully. 'If you want everlasting life, you try praying.'

Mr G. Hayman took out a purse of money and placed it in front of Mrs Smith. 'Please,' she said. 'Did he ever mention it?'

She took the purse and tucked it away. 'He say he lived many lives, this man. He seen more years than you and me. He call himself an old soul.'

'You mean he had performed the Eternity Spell? It really is possible,' whispered Lord Ringmore.

'So he say.' Mrs Smith nodded. 'But this man, he not a happy man. He say a long life different to a happy life.'

'Did he give some indication of how it could be done? A clue, anything?' asked Lord Ringmore.

'I not ask,' said Mrs Smith. 'I not want to know about such things. What I told you is all I know about that. You ask me, the only folk who want to cheat death are the ones that feel cheated by death themselves. Ain't that right, Lord?'

The interview over, Mr G. Hayman and Lord Ringmore emerged from the house to find hoards of ragged, skinny children gathered around to stare, but none were foolish enough to come within striking distance of Lord Ringmore's walking stick.

'Cheated by death?' said Mr G. Hayman, as they stepped into the sanctuary of a hansom cab. 'Is that how you feel?'

Lord Ringmore kept his eyes fixed ahead. 'I was eleven years old when it happened,' he said. 'My father's condition had grown steadily worse. Some days he was unnervingly affectionate, others he barely knew me or he got me confused with some dead family member. One night, after a sustained period of this, I awoke. It was late but I was thirsty so I went downstairs to fetch a glass of water. I heard Roud, my father's personal butler, in the kitchen. He was talking to the scullery maid, making her laugh with stories of things the old man had said and done that day. I was furious, of course. The man was a scoundrel. Resolving to tell Mother the next day and have him dismissed, I turned to go back to bed and saw my father standing in his nightgown at the top of the stairs.'

'He had heard too?' asked Mr G. Hayman.

'No, I don't think so. At that stage, he rarely understood anything anyway but he looked at me and spoke my name. I was relieved to hear him say it. Each time he lost his memory I feared it would never return. Then he said something I will never forget. "Silas," he said, "death comes to us all sooner or later."'

'True enough words,' said Mr G. Hayman. The carriage rattled on over the uneven, cobbled street.

'Before I could ask what he meant, he let go of the bannister and allowed himself to fall forward. By the time he reached the bottom he was dead.'

'That's terrible,' said Mr G. Hayman.

'My mother lived another year or so. After that, I was alone.'

'I'm so sorry.' Mr G. Hayman placed a gloved hand over Lord Ringmore's, but he moved it away.

'We need to keep an eye on Clay,' he said. 'You and I have believed for a long time, but his world has been rocked by these discoveries. I have seen that look in his eyes. He would take this gift, slap a bow tie on it and put it on the stage. It is too valuable to be squandered on theatricals.'

'I'll talk to him,' replied Mr G. Hayman.

40

Spitalfields

Tom had first come across the hiding place in Spitalfields by scaling the side of the market wall and finding a space above a coffee shack. It was a good spot and perfectly hidden from sight. The noises of the market and smells from the coffee shack were comforting. Unlike the crypt it was airy, and a pleasant place to while away a few hours.

Esther was already there when Tom arrived. He instantly sensed the difference in her.

'I knew you would do it,' said Tom.

Esther stared back at him. 'What have we done, Tom?' she asked, quietly. 'What have we become?'

'More than we were.' He sat down and took her hand. 'Things will be good from now on, Est. You'll see. Look, I'm better now.' He pulled back his sleeve to reveal that the warts had vanished from his arm.

'Everything feels different,' said Esther.

'Of course it does,' said Tom. 'And we can say goodbye

to hide-spots like this. From now on, people will need to hide from us.'

'It's all happening too quickly,' said Esther.

'What's wrong with you?'

'I saw Hardy. He said the police are looking for us.'

Tom's eyes drifted down to the wart on her hand. 'What did you do to him?'

'I don't know. It wasn't me. I didn't feel in control. I'm not in control.'

'Well, I am. I know exactly what I'm doing.'

'And what of *him*?' Esther pointed up at the market roof.

'Who?'

'Mondriat. He's sitting up there spying on us, listening to everything we say.'

Tom saw the mangy magpie poke his head out from behind a rafter then come fluttering down.

'Where have you been?' asked Tom.

'I've been learning,' said Mondriat. 'And I'd like to have a look at the book, if you don't mind.'

Esther stared at the magpie. After all that had happened it shouldn't have been a shock to hear it speak but it was still very strange.

'Yes, yes, yes, I can talk,' said the magpie. 'And funnily enough my name isn't Mister Magpie, so don't even think about it. Now, where's the book?'

'It's gone,' admitted Esther.

'Gone?' squawked the magpie.

'What? You let Hardy take it?' said Tom.

'No. Someone else. I don't know who. I was distracted.

What's it matter anyway? Like you said, we can create our own spells now.'

'It matters because that book was written by Olwyn Broe,' said Mondriat.

'Who?' asked Esther.

'Olwyn was the most complicated, beautiful woman I ever met and the most gifted Conjuress to ever cast a spell. Olwyn could imagine the most extraordinary things. She would create the most beautiful Conjury I've ever seen. She could even manipulate time itself. What I wouldn't give to see her again.' The magpie sighed. 'That can never happen. She will never forgive me for something I did, many centuries ago. But I can still, at least, see her spells. You'll just have to get the book back.'

'I've got something else to do first,' said Tom. 'I'm going to find my aunt.'

'Your aunt left you on the doorstep of the orphanage when you were five years old,' said Esther.

'Because she couldn't afford to bring me up,' said Tom. 'Things are different now.'

'When people leave children at the orphanage they don't want them to come looking for them,' said Esther.

'I knew you wouldn't understand. You never had any family like me.'

Esther stared furiously back at Tom.

'I'm sorry,' said Tom. 'But it's something I have to do.'

'We should get out of London, Tom,' said Esther. 'We can leave and start again. We don't need to be us any more.'

'So you won't help me find her?'

'No, she won't,' said Mondriat. 'She has to find a mirror before she does anything, but I'll help you, Tom. I know the perfect potion to help find her. Then after that we can go and find the book.'

'You're not going to listen to him?' said Esther.

'Go find a mirror,' said Tom.

Esther noticed Tom's staff. It was the same stick as before, except it had been painted black, its rough edges sanded down and a gold handle fixed to the top. 'What's happening to you, Tom?'

'I'm bettering myself,' he replied.

41

Immortality

When Fred opened the door, he found Clay holding in his arms a bundle of clothes, caked in mud. His face and hands were splattered too, giving him the appearance of a creature that had crawled from the depths of hell to be there.

'I won't ask,' said Fred.

'Better not to,' agreed Clay. 'Dispose of these, will you?'

Clay handed the clothes to Fred who held them at arm's length. 'For me? You shouldn't have.'

'I'm all heart.'

'You have a visitor,' said Fred.

'A visitor?'

'There's a *gentleman* awaiting your return in the library,' said Fred. 'Wouldn't take no for an answer.'

The reason for Fred's emphasis on the word *gentleman* became apparent when Mr G. Hayman stepped out of the library.

'Mud bath, Clay?' she said.

'Not exactly. To what do I owe this pleasure?' asked Clay. He kicked off his muddy shoes and led her back into the room, carefully opening a dresser drawer and extracting a tea towel as he did so.

'Our lines of work are not so different, you know,' said Mr G. Hayman. 'Our audiences applaud not for the danger we have shown them but out of relief that it is over.'

'I thought you were going to say that we both deceive in the name of money and art,' replied Clay.

Mr G. Hayman ran her fingers over the spines of the books that lined the wall. 'Should I be offended that I see none of my titles here?' she asked.

'I prefer books that tell you something.'

'It seems to me the line between fiction and fact is often unclear.'

'You'll excuse me if I fail to see any purpose in all this.'

'Over many years of painstaking research I have heard again and again of a spell, which, if cast in the right circumstances, will deliver the gift of immortality. It is known as the Eternity Spell.'

Both of them fell silent as Fred entered the room with a tea tray, placed it down and left.

Clay spooned two sugars into a cup of tea and downed it in one gulp. 'As fascinating as all this is, I have preparations to make. My run at the Theatre Royal begins in a couple of nights.'

'Did you get the book, Clay?' asked Mr G. Hayman.

'With every police officer searching London you think *I* managed to –'

'Please don't treat me as a fool,' she warned sternly. 'You have the book.'

'What makes you say that?'

'I know people, Clay. Even slippery ones like you. You knew why I was here the moment Fred informed you and yet you were happy to dance around the subject. If you didn't have it, you would have asked me to come to the point much sooner.'

'Maybe I just enjoy dancing with you,' replied Clay.

'You think you want this book more than any of us, don't you?'

Clay poured himself another cup of tea. 'What would I want with a magic book?'

'You think that with real magic you will be able to create an act that no one could copy. You fear all these new performers. They are young, hungry and willing to push the boundaries. You fear that soon you will be an antiquated irrelevance or else that the next time you plunge into the water you will never come back out.'

'I didn't realise you listed mind-reading amongst your many talents.'

'It's not mind-reading. This is a skill we refer to as empathy.'

'You novelists?' said Clay.

'Us women,' said Mr G. Hayman.

Clay laughed.

'But you're wrong,' she continued. 'You are not the one who desires it the most. No one could want this more than Lord Ringmore. He knows we can use it to learn the secret of the Eternity Spell. Immortality, Clay. Living forever, not living on in memory but in actuality.'

Clay laughed. 'You are not serious.'

'Perhaps. Perhaps not, but you have to admit it's intriguing. Even if you could unlock the secrets of the book without us, you would squander this gift on entertainment when you could stay loyal to us and uncover the truth about the Eternity Spell. The book is the key but you need someone to show you the lock.' She stood so close to Clay he could feel her breath on his face. Something about the way her eyes flickered with excitement kept him rooted to the spot. It was rare for Clay to feel so unnerved. He enjoyed the feeling.

Clay turned around and pulled open the drawer from which he had taken the tea towel. There, slipped inside, without his guest having seen, was the book. He lifted it out and handed it to her.

42

Pain

Children rarely returned to St Clement's Catholic School for Waifs and Strays to say thank you. Mother Agnes expected no gratitude for having dedicated her life to their well-being. The knowledge that she was doing the Lord's work was thanks enough for her. The Lord had taken their parents from them and delivered them to the orphanage, where there was no place for any love other than His own. And God's love was a hard love. Of that, Mother Agnes had no doubt. She tried to ensure that all her orphans grew up fearing God, but the boy who sat in her office, awaiting her return, had never shown fear of anything at all.

'I'm afraid I'm very busy,' said Mother Agnes. 'I can only spare a couple of minutes if that.' She tapped a pile of papers on her desk by way of explanation.

'Not too busy for me though, eh? You always had a little time for Hardy in your office, didn't you?'

'That is not the name I gave you,' she replied curtly.

'No,' he agreed.

None of the orphans at St Clement's were afforded the opportunity to grow fat but, with his broad shoulders, thick neck and large hands, Hardy had always been larger than most.

'*Quiet reflection*,' he said.

Mother Agnes met his stare. She was determined not to be intimidated by this child. 'I told you, I don't have much time now –' she started.

'Where is it?' Hardy interrupted.

'I don't know what you –'

'Where is it?' he repeated.

'Quiet reflection was supposed to help you become a better person. I fear it did not work with you.'

'Don't worry, I'm not here for revenge,' said Hardy. 'It's just that while I'm here I'd like to see it again.'

Slowly, Mother Agnes opened the top drawer of her desk and pulled out a heavy wooden ruler. The inch marks were worn away and one end was rough and splintered from a thousand beatings. Mother Agnes was surprised to see Hardy's eyes moisten at the sight of it.

He leaned forward and whispered hoarsely, 'It was a joke, wasn't it?'

'How dare you question my methods?' replied Mother Agnes.

'It was a joke,' he said emphatically. 'The others screamed, didn't they? I heard them. With each scream they learnt about quiet reflection.' He chuckled. 'A *sick* joke at that.'

'It is an important lesson.'

'What lesson? You wanted us to learn how to suffer in silence?'

'Life *is* suffering,' snapped the prioress. 'Would it not be better if everyone could learn to suffer in silence? God demands our praise. He does not want to hear our petty moans.'

Hardy chuckled. 'It's actually funny now I think on it. Quiet reflection.'

'You never made a sound,' said Mother Agnes. 'Why not?'

'I didn't want to give you the satisfaction,' replied Hardy.

'Your behaviour caused you a lot of unnecessary pain.'

'Unnecessary, you say?'

'I needed to break your will,' snapped Mother Agnes. 'I was trying to beat the devil out of you. It was for your own good.'

'Ah, but you only ended up pushing him further down inside of me.'

'Do not speak of your work with him! This is a good, charitable institution. It is a place of God.'

Hardy opened his palm. 'Try me now,' he said.

'Now, please . . .' Mother Agnes blushed.

'Do it,' repeated Hardy.

'I will not be –'

'Do it now or I'll tear that thing from your hand and give you some quiet reflection of your own,' said Hardy.

The prioress brought the ruler down on his hand, cracking the hard wood against his skin.

He didn't flinch. 'Again,' he said.

She hit him harder, leaving a red mark across his palm. Hardy's eyes were dry now. She didn't need to be told again. She hit him a third time. More than anything she wanted a reaction. She needed a reaction. It was all she had ever wanted from him. She brought the ruler down a fourth time. A fifth, sixth and seventh. Still Hardy said nothing.

'No more,' said Mother Agnes, at last.

'You want to know my secret?' said Hardy. 'I enjoy the pain. That's what you taught me: the ability to dish out pain gives you real power. Except over people like me, that is.'

'You wicked child,' said Mother Agnes. She swung the ruler again, but this time Hardy caught it and yanked it out of her hand. 'God watches everything you do,' she yelled. 'You can't escape His judgement!'

'God's a thief and a coward,' said Hardy. 'God's a tyrant and a liar.'

'You *dare* to blaspheme?'

'Pain is my god,' said Hardy. 'You taught me that too.'

'Why are you here?' asked Mother Agnes, breathlessly.

'Tom and Esther,' said Hardy. 'Where are they?'

'I'm sure I don't know, but you aren't the first to come searching for them.'

'The law?'

'No. A man by the name of Harry Clay.'

'I've heard that name.'

'He came here two days ago.'

'What did you tell him?'

'I told him the same thing I'm telling you. I have no idea

where they went. I have not seen either of them since they left.'

Hardy stood up, still holding the ruler. 'I think I'll keep this,' he said.

'You would steal from an orphanage?' said Mother Agnes.

'Steal? I've earned this.' Hardy tucked the ruler into his belt and left.

43

Reclamation

There was a palpable feeling of anxiety in the air as the four remaining members of the Society of Thirteen gathered once more in the club library.

'I heard this morning that the coroner confirms that Symmonds died of natural causes,' said Sir Tyrrell. 'The police are no longer looking for the Indian.'

'It's a terrible business,' said Mr G. Hayman. 'Poor John.'

'John's death is a tragedy but we should not allow it to distract us from the matter in hand,' said Lord Ringmore, coldly.

'I'm afraid Inspector Longdale has not yet recovered the book,' said Sir Tyrrell.

'And yet, as a result of the police's actions, Harry was able to lay his hands on it.' Lord Ringmore pulled the book out from a pocket in his coat and placed it on a table.

'Longdale set a bunch of thugs after them,' said Clay. 'They provided an excellent distraction. This time I saw the girl turn the mud from the riverbed into a weapon. The power they wield is remarkable. It could create a stage show the like of which the world has never seen before.'

'A stage show –?' barked Sir Tyrrell.

'Thankfully,' interrupted Lord Ringmore, 'Mr Hayman was on hand to rescue the book from such an inconsequential fate and remind Harry where his loyalties lie.'

'We all have our agendas, don't we, Ringmore?' said Clay.

'Well, *some* of us would use this power to better the world,' said Sir Tyrrell. 'So, what now? We know we need a thirteen-year-old without parents, but what must we have them do?'

'My research has revealed the answer,' explained Mr G. Hayman. 'The child uses a wand or staff to make a shape in the ground. When they step inside that shape the lifeblood infects them.'

'Have you learnt what shape it is?' asked Clay.

'Yes. Going back through my notes, I realised that the answer has been right in front of us since the beginning,' said Mr G. Hayman. She flipped the book around to show the symbol on the back. 'This shape. The circle within the triangle within the circle. This is the Creation Spell, gentlemen.'

Clay clapped his hands together in excitement. 'Then all we need is a subject.'

'I have a nephew of thirteen. He would be perfect. He was orphaned following the death of my dear brother last year,' said Sir Tyrrell. 'I've been like a father to the boy ever since.'

'Can he be trusted?' asked Mr G. Hayman.

'He is a Tyrrell and therefore totally trustworthy.'

'And yet there are now two children out there who are already wielding such power,' said Lord Ringmore. 'If we are to control this power we must first contain it. We must draw the orphans back to us.'

'A Conjuror of our own will give us bargaining power,' mused Clay.

'I agree,' said Mr G. Hayman.

'As do I,' added Sir Tyrrell.

'Very well, then we will try out your nephew first then use him to entice the orphans back,' said Lord Ringmore.

44

Blood

Mondriat led Tom to a patch of wasteland between two factories that churned out smoke from huge chimneys. In the summer there was probably enough grass to call it a park but in the winter it was abandoned and desolate, save for a few stray dogs.

'If you want to locate your aunt, you must create a hunting potion,' explained the magpie.

'A potion? Why not a spell?'

'Spells can harness great power, but a potion is more potent, as it draws out the essence of the lifeblood itself.'

'What ingredients do we need?'

Mondriat laughed. 'You think we need a bubbling cauldron and eyes of a newt, I suppose?'

'No,' said Tom. 'It's just . . . what then?'

'First, you must dig your cauldron.' Mondriat tapped his beak on the ground.

'It's frozen solid. How can I dig?'

'You hold the answer in your right hand,' replied Mondriat.

Tom looked at his staff.

'With this?' he said.

'With that.'

Tom tried to ram his staff into the ground but it barely made any impact at all.

'What are you doing?' squawked Mondriat. 'You're a Conjuror! When I say to use your staff, I mean use it as a staff, not as a stick. Use your power, your strength. Find a spell within you that will create the cauldron in the earth.'

Tom nodded and placed both hands on one end of the staff. He knelt down and moved it instinctively in a spiralling motion. He could feel the raw energy rise up through it. He closed his eyes as though in prayer. The staff vibrated and, when Tom opened his eyes, he saw it had created a perfectly circular hole in the ground.

'Not bad for your first attempt,' said Mondriat. 'Now, draw the Creation Spell around the cauldron.'

As Tom completed the final line he felt the power pulsate from the ground.

'The Creation Spell is the basis of all magic,' said Mondriat. 'The circle summons the illuminated energy, the triangle harnesses shaded energy.'

'There is good and bad magic?' said Tom.

'Good and bad are words used by unInfected souls. A dog may be good or bad. A song may be good or bad. We are not talking about dogs or music. The energy of the Earthsoul, shaded or illuminated, is beautiful.'

'So how do I make a potion?'

'A potion requires liquid. Blood, in fact. Your blood, to be precise.'

'My blood?' said Tom, alarmed.

'Just one droplet of your own, exquisitely Infected blood. You'll barely notice it.'

'Is there a spell to draw out my blood?'

'Some things you don't need magic for.'

Before Tom could ask what Mondriat meant, he flew onto his arm and jabbed his beak into Tom's hand.

'Hey!' protested Tom, pulling his hand away to see that Mondriat had pierced his skin and that a droplet of blood glistened on his palm.

Mondriat fluttered up to the safety of a nearby tree. 'Now hold your hand over the cauldron and allow the blood to drip in.'

Tom scowled at him but followed his instructions, allowing two drops to fall into the hole then sucking the wound dry. As the red droplets hit the centre of the hole they hissed like eggs hitting a hot frying pan. Red liquid oozed from the pores of the earth, filling the hole. White steam rose from the surface of the potion.

'How will this help me find my aunt?' asked Tom.

'The Earthsoul knows all,' said Mondriat. 'The lifeblood held in this cauldron contains all of time and space. The past dwells with the present. The present mixes with the future. Nothing is impossible and no question is unanswerable, but the answers must come from within.'

'Meaning?'

'You must drink the potion.'

'Drink it?' said Tom. 'Drink my own blood?'

'This is not your blood,' replied Mondriat. 'This is a potion made from the pure moisture of the Earthsoul. You must drink it then hold the question in your mind.'

'I have no cup.'

'The cup,' said Mondriat, hopping along the branch. 'I always did forget the cup.'

Tom dropped to his knees and crawled tentatively towards the bubbling liquid. It smelt strange. He cupped his hands and lifted a handful of the liquid to his mouth.

To his surprise, it was the most exquisite thing he had ever tasted. He lapped up more, then dropped down and pushed his head into the hole, not caring that the liquid splashed around his face. He greedily guzzled it down. When he had drained the hole of every drop he rolled over and looked up at the overcast sky. Mondriat was speaking but he could no longer hear what he was saying. The clouds shifted, creating shapes as the bright sun eagerly sought a way through. These were the shapes of nature. This was the Earthsoul speaking. The clouds swirled around and formed a child's face he knew to be his mother. He watched her age and grow. A second figure appeared, a faceless man who took Tom's mother in his arms. Tom wanted to cry out but there was a flash of light and the sound of screaming. His mother reappeared, alone again. He watched her belly swell as a child inside grew. With another dramatic swirl of clouds, she was holding the baby in her arms. The baby became a boy and he recognised himself, but the image of his mother faded into the background and he saw his aunt standing behind him in her place. She placed a hand on his shoulder and led him away.

Tears obscured Tom's vision. The image moved further and further away, as though he was flying up into the sky, until he looked down on London. He saw the curve of the river, the living snake-heart of the city. Forever flowing. He saw every living, breathing thing, moving like ants on the ground, going about their business, unaware of their insignificance. Tom could have identified the position of anyone or anything, but there was only one who mattered.

Tom sat upright and looked at Mondriat.

'Well?' asked Mondriat.

'I know where she is,' he replied.

45

Pendant

Esther had always been quick on her feet, but now, with every sense heightened, she could have navigated the busy market with her eyes closed. The calls of the stall-owners echoed in her ears. Whereas once she had taken great comfort from such hustle and bustle, today it only reminded her of her isolation.

She stopped next to a fruit stall where a woman was carefully considering every piece of fruit in minute detail, much to the stall-owner's annoyance. Esther noticed her purse poking out of her basket. Taking it would have been the easiest thing in the world. Even without magic Esther could have snatched it and vanished into the throng before the woman knew it was gone.

The woman turned around and saw her standing behind her. Esther saw the flash of fear in her eyes as she looked for her purse and the relief that swept across her face when she found it still there.

Esther left the market and walked up Bushfield Street where there were more stalls, selling jewellery, brushes and combs, snuff tins and other knick-knacks. She approached one filled with silver and gold necklaces. The owner was an oriental lady wearing an exotic red and gold blouse.

'You see something you like?' she said.

Esther's eyes were drawn to a necklace with a delicate silver chain and a hanging pendant.

'You like this one?' said the stall-owner.

'I don't know,' replied Esther.

'This one is very special necklace. Look.' The stall-owner pressed the side of the pendant and it clicked open. 'Inside you can put a picture of a loved one . . . or leave as is.'

The lady turned it around to reveal a tiny mirror inside.

'Take a look.' She handed the necklace to her. She showed no concern that Esther might run away with it. 'No one is as important as the one you see in there.'

'How much is it?' asked Esther.

'For you, special price. For you, five shillings,' said the woman.

Ever since Hardy had counted out the money earned from the robbery of Lord Ringmore's house she had wanted rid of it. It was a reminder of the betrayal. There was no question of haggling for a better price.

She paid and the oriental lady handed her the necklace. 'It will bring you luck.'

Esther put the chain over her neck then tucked the pendant out of sight. She felt its coldness against her skin as she headed towards Brick Lane. There, she found a quiet corner where there was no one around and pulled out the pendant. When she opened it she saw her face reflected in the tiny mirror. There had been no mirrors in the orphanage. Mother Agnes had called them 'windows of vanity'. Esther looked into her own eyes, so unfamiliar, so strange, and so full of fear. In her right hand, she felt her staff move, scratching the shapes into the dirt.

The world melted around her. Or was it she who was melting? For a moment, Esther was utterly alone, then, she saw a woman standing where her reflection had been. She had dark hair and eyes as black as the night. She stared back at Esther. She scrutinised her. She examined her.

'Who are you? demanded Esther.

The woman did not reply but threw her head back and laughed. Frightened, Esther stepped back, stumbled and tripped.

'You all right, love?'

She was back in the street again, sitting on the ground. A cloth-capped man, pushing a large cart of lemons, had stopped upon seeing her fall.

'Don't touch me,' she warned.

'Only being friendly, weren't I?' he replied.

Esther stared at him until he shrugged, mumbled something under his breath and walked away.

Her hand found the pendant. It was still open. She lifted it again and looked into the mirror. This time she saw only her own face reflected. The dark-haired woman, whoever she was, had gone from the mirror, but the sound of her laughter still rang in Esther's ears and the image of her face remained imprinted on her memory. She looked at the back of her hand. The wart had gone. She snapped the pendant shut and tucked it out of sight.

46

Collapse

The vision in the clouds had revealed to Tom that his aunt lived in a cosy-looking cottage, halfway up Highgate Hill, with a small neat garden and flowers in the window. It was not what he had expected. He knew his aunt had only given him up because she couldn't afford to keep him, so how could she be living in such a place?

Tom had felt groggy after drinking the potion, but the journey across London gave him time to clear his head. Mondriat had respected Tom's wishes and was keeping his distance. He landed on the cottage roof as Tom pushed open the gate and walked up the path.

A neighbour, washing her doorstep, stood up to peer over the fence. Tom stared back until she looked away and returned to her work.

When he banged on the door a baby started crying inside.

'Who is it?' cried a female voice.

Tom didn't know how to answer, so he said nothing and knocked again.

'Hold on. I'm coming.' His aunt's voice was harsher than he remembered, but he was in no doubt that it was her.

The door opened and she appeared, exactly as she had looked in the vision, except that she held in her arms a screaming child. 'Yes?' she said, eyeing him suspiciously.

'I –' Tom began.

'It had better be important,' she interrupted. 'I'll never get her down again now you've woken her up.'

'I'm Tom.'

'Tom? I don't know any Toms. Are you one of them kids from number thirty-nine? Locked yourself out, have you?'

'I'm your nephew, Tom,' he said.

'My nephew . . .' She laughed at first, but slowly the laughter fell away and the colour drained from her face. 'Good God. How the devil did you find me?'

'Does it matter how?' asked Tom.

'It matters to me,' she snapped. 'They said you wouldn't be able to find me. They promised.'

'Things have changed now,' said Tom. 'I've changed. I can look after us now.'

The baby choked on its own screams. 'Don't be so stupid, child. I don't need you to look after us. I've got a family. Can't you see?'

A boy appeared by her legs, staring sullenly at Tom. 'Who is it, Mummy?' he asked.

'No one,' replied his aunt.

'I ain't no one,' said Tom.

'You can't be here,' she said. 'My Charlie will be back soon. He won't want to find you here and you don't want to be found here by him, neither.'

'I understand why you had to leave me,' said Tom. 'You couldn't afford to keep me, but it'll be all right now. We're family.'

'I left you because Charlie didn't want to bring up my sister's runt. And why should he? I did what I could for you.'

'You washed your hands of me!' exclaimed Tom.

'And now you're back, knocking on my door, making a scene.'

The neighbour had stopped all pretence of scrubbing the doorstep and was blatantly staring over the fence at the scene.

'Who is he, Mummy?' asked the little boy.

'I told you. He's no one,' said Tom's aunt.

Tom looked at the child. 'I'm your cousin, Tom.'

'Don't you listen to him.'

'How old is he?' asked Tom.

'Never you mind.'

'I am five,' said the boy, proudly.

It was the age Tom had been when his aunt had left him on the doorstep of the orphanage. The anger bubbled up inside of him. Esther had been right all along. His aunt didn't want him. She had never wanted him. Raw pain tore at his insides.

The boy was crying now too.

'What you doing with that stick?' demanded his aunt.

Tom looked at his right hand. His staff was moving.

'When my Charlie gets here . . .' The rest of his aunt's threat was drowned out by the blood pounding in Tom's ears. 'There was always something wrong about you . . .' she said. 'I was glad Charlie made me give you away . . . You hear that, Tom? Glad.'

Tom looked at his aunt with renewed clarity. He raised his left hand and touched the doorframe. The shaking that had filled his body moved through his fingertips into the walls of the cottage. His aunt looked up, terrified, as the building began to shake. On the roof, Mondriat flapped his wings and flew to a nearby tree.

'What've you done, Tom? What you done?' demanded his aunt. She pushed past him, holding the baby in one arm and dragging the other child behind her.

'Goodbye.' Tom turned to leave. He didn't need to stay to watch the huge cracks snake through the building, sending shards of glass flying from the cracked windows. He didn't need to see the building crumble to dust while the children screamed and the neighbours rushed out to stare. He didn't need to take in the magnificence of what he had done. Why would he need to see it when he had so perfectly imagined it?

47

Split

By the time Esther arrived on Highgate Hill, clouds of dust were billowing out from the collapsed cottage. All around, people were coming out of houses and shops to witness the spectacle but, in spite of the hysterical cries from Tom's aunt, no one believed that the cause of the disaster was the thirteen-year-old boy walking away.

Esther stood in front of him, blocking his way, searching his face for a sign of remorse.

'She deserves no better,' said Tom, before she could say a word.

'We both got left, but we found each other, didn't we?' replied Esther.

'It's not the same.'

'You can't swap lives with anyone else. The way it is for you is the way it is,' said Esther.

'I know.'

'Then no more of this. Please. That woman, she ain't

your family any more. You and me, we're the only family we got.'

Behind them, the crowds were finally taking notice of this woman's hysterical cries and turning to look at Tom.

'Come on, let's go,' said Tom.

A bus was rumbling past, heading down Highgate Hill. The orphans ran after it, leaping onto the back and hitching a ride as far as Archway, where they jumped off and continued on foot.

'We can both do as we want from now on,' said Tom. 'We can finally live how we always dreamed we would. Better even. We'll have it all.'

'It scares me when you talk like that,' said Esther.

'Did you see those people's faces? If folks are scared of you they'll give you most anything.'

'I don't want anyone to be scared of me,' said Esther.

'Well, I do,' replied Tom.

'Is that why you destroyed the cottage?' asked Esther. 'Because you want your aunt to fear you? You want her children to grow up having nightmares about you?'

A well-dressed nanny, pushing a pram, nervously glanced at them as she passed.

Tom noticed Esther's wart-free hand. 'You've done the Mirror Spell?'

'Yes. But it wasn't me. I saw another face, a woman I didn't recognise. I don't know what it meant. It scared me. All of this scares me. We have to get out before it's too late,' Esther told Tom. 'We should leave this city, get away from Hardy and Ringmore. Leave the lot of them behind. That's why I came to find you.'

Tom stopped dead as a thought struck him. 'How did you find me?'

'You ain't exactly hard to find. You destroyed a house, Tom,' replied Esther.

'I could have been anywhere in London.'

'What's it matter?'

'How did you find me, Esther?' he repeated.

Esther tried to look away but she knew she had to tell him the truth. If they had any chance of starting afresh she had to be honest. 'I knew where your aunt lived because I overheard Mother Agnes one night. It was after you'd been misbehaving. She said to one of the other nuns that she had a good mind to drag you up Highgate Hill and deliver you back to your aunt's doorstep.'

'You never told me,' Tom whispered.

'Like I said, when people leave children at the orphanage they don't want to see them again. None of them,' said Esther.

'You knew.' This time Tom screamed the words, drawing the attention of more people passing by.

'I didn't know any more than that. Please, Tom. I didn't tell you because I didn't want you to get hurt. Look what happened when you found her. I told you no good would come of it.'

'Yeah, you told me just like you tell me everything. But things have changed. No one gets to tell me what to do any more. Not the nuns, not Ringmore, not Hardy, not you.'

'We need to stick together.'

'All this time, and you never told me,' said Tom. 'I can't forgive you for that.'

The orphans stood glowering at each other, clutching their staffs. Esther understood that all was lost now. Tom's eyes revealed pure hatred. As far as he was concerned, she had betrayed him. She may as well be dead. Esther moved her staff in the dust and vanished into thin air.

48

Cyril

Sir Augustus Tyrrell spent precious little time in his inherited family home. The mansion was unnecessarily large for his bachelor needs and, for such a confirmed city dweller, the seemingly endless acres of Sussex countryside that surrounded it were terrifically dull. It was only its proximity to his nephew's boarding school that made him suggest it as a suitable location for the next meeting.

As the remaining Society members stood on the steps in front of the grand building, Clay pointed out that the approaching coach had a distinct lean, the cause of which was revealed when Sir Tyrrell's nephew stepped out.

'Cyril, my boy,' said Sir Tyrrell. 'How very kind of you to join us.'

'Hello, Uncle Gus,' said the boy.

'The boy's name is Cyril Tyrrell,' Mr G. Hayman muttered in Clay's ear, making him smirk.

'I say, Uncle, what's all this about?' asked Cyril. 'It's quite a welcoming party!'

'Let's call it a scientific experiment,' replied Sir Tyrrell, patting his nephew's back affectionately.

'I should hope it is important. I'm having to miss Sports for this.'

'You like sports?' asked Clay, glancing at Mr G. Hayman.

'I like boxing,' replied Cyril. 'Say, I know you! You're Harry Clay. I went to see your show last Christmas.'

Clay bowed graciously.

'Very amusing, I must say, but I saw through every one of your tricks,' said the boy. 'It's all stooges and trapdoors, isn't it?'

'What a sharp-minded boy you are,' said Clay, through gritted teeth.

'Do you have a show on at the moment?'

'Once we are done here I'm taking the train back to London for the first night of my new run.'

'Perhaps I'll come to that one too.'

'Please let me know if you can come along,' said Clay. 'You could come up on stage and look for trapdoors. Maybe I could make you disappear.'

Lord Ringmore laughed and placed a hand on Clay's shoulder. 'Come now,' he said. 'Let's to our business.'

'Does our business involve cake?' asked Cyril, walking up the stairs to the front door. 'I'm famished.'

'You can eat after we are done,' said Lord Ringmore, 'but our experiment will be conducted outside.'

Lord Ringmore led them onto the lawn.

'First the boy should choose his wand,' said Mr G. Hayman.

'A wand?' said Cyril, with a snigger.

'Any branch should do,' said Mr G. Hayman. 'It needs to be something that grew from the earth itself but long and sturdy enough to form the Creation Spell.'

Cyril laughed. 'I say, what's going on, Uncle Gus? Is this some kind of joke?'

'Please,' said Sir Tyrrell. 'All will become apparent. Just do as we say.'

'How about this?' Clay picked up a branch from beside a sycamore tree and handed it to Cyril. 'How does that feel?'

'Very much like a branch,' replied the boy.

'Good, then we are ready,' said Lord Ringmore.

'Now what do I do?' asked Cyril.

Mr G. Hayman held up the book. 'You must make this shape on the ground,' she said, pointing out the shape on the back of the book.

'What do you mean, make the shape?'

'With the branch, boy,' snapped Lord Ringmore. 'Scratch out the shape on the ground.'

'But it's frozen solid.'

'That doesn't matter,' said Mr G. Hayman. 'The shape will still draw the power of the Earthsoul.'

'The what?' blurted Cyril.

'Just do it, please,' snapped Lord Ringmore, anxiously.

'All right, keep your hat on,' replied the boy.

Concentrating hard, he drew the shape of a circle within a triangle within a circle.

'You must stand at the centre of the inner circle to make

the Creation Spell work,' said Mr G. Hayman.

The others watched tensely as Cyril completed the shape and stepped inside. 'Well. What now?'

'How do you feel?' asked Sir Tyrrell.

'Hungry,' replied Cyril.

'How should he feel?' asked Lord Ringmore.

'I don't know,' replied Mr G. Hayman.

'I have to say, I'm beginning to think even Mr Clay's tricks are better than this one,' said Cyril.

'I don't understand,' said Mr G. Hayman. 'We performed the Creation Spell with an orphaned boy of thirteen. It should have worked.'

'Did you say thirteen?' asked Cyril.

'Yes, yes, thirteen. Your age,' replied Sir Tyrrell

'I turned fourteen just last month, Uncle Gus,' said Cyril. 'Cook gave me double helpings of puddings. I really rather wish I had more than just the one birthday per year if I get double helpings every time.'

'Fourteen?' exploded Lord Ringmore.

'Are you sure?' asked Sir Tyrrell.

'I think the boy knows his own age.' Clay sighed.

'Say, if we're done I'd really appreciate something along the lines of a cake before I head back to school,' said Cyril.

'Yes, we are done here.' Lord Ringmore spun around and stormed back to the house.

49

Heritage

Esther had been walking for hours, unsure where to go or what to do, when she became aware of the black cat following her. She waited until no one was around before she stopped and spun around to face it.

'What do you want? Who are you?' she demanded.

'What makes you think I'm not just a cat?' replied the cat.

'You're the same one that appeared in Bedford Square. You chased Mondriat away. Then you turned up in Rotherhithe. Now you're here.' Esther looked closely at the cat, thinking carefully. 'You're her, aren't you? You're Olwyn.'

'That was once a name I used, yes.'

'Why are you following me?' asked Esther.

'I want to help you. Just as Mondriat is Tom's familiar, I could be yours,' purred Olwyn. 'I can show you how to do great things.'

'I don't want to do great things.'

'Yes, but the thing is, Esther, you are my responsibility.'

'I don't understand.'

'I'm going to tell you a story,' said the cat. 'It's about a pair of young Conjurors, many centuries ago, very much in love and with the whole world at their feet. They were so happy that they wanted to be like that forever. They didn't want their happiness to end. They didn't want to succumb to death, so they set about looking for a solution. They went in search of the secrets of the Eternity Spell.'

'You're talking about yourself,' said Esther.

'Myself and Mondriat.'

'The two of you were together?'

The cat bowed her head. 'As we searched for the spell that would conquer death, Mondriat came to believe that the solution lay not in creation, but in destruction. He decided that it would take strength to achieve that which we sought and so he set about stealing others' Conjury.'

'How can Conjury be stolen?'

'Mirror theft,' said Olwyn. 'Mondriat stole Conjury from mirror after mirror.'

'Did it work?'

'It certainly made him stronger and it ended countless Conjurors' lives but no, this is not the way to achieve immortality. Unwittingly, Mondriat helped the brutal witch-hunters bring about the end of Conjury.'

'Why are you telling me this?'

'Because you need to see that he cannot be trusted.'

'But what has it to do with me?'

'Esther, please, I'm trying to explain something. I want to tell you about how your mother died.'

At the mention of her mother, Esther felt a tug on her heart. She felt tears form in her eyes but she pushed them back inside. This was no time to cry. She needed to understand what Olwyn was saying. 'These events. You said, they were hundreds of years ago.'

'A hundred years is no more than a blink of an eye to the Earthsoul.'

'Was my mother a Conjuress too?' asked Esther.

The cat shook her head. 'She was an innocent peasant whose only mistake was to take pity on a Conjuress in fear of her life. Me, Esther. She took me in while the angry witch-hunting mobs pursued me. Unfortunately, and to my eternal regret, her association with me was enough to convince them that she was a witch. The trial was short, the punishment brutal and final.'

'You mean, they killed her?'

'I was unable to stop them and I knew that they would kill her child too if they had the chance, so I cast a spell and sent you somewhere I hoped you would be safe.'

'Where?'

'Into the folds of time, Esther. I sent you into the future so that you might live.'

Before she had cast the Creation Spell, Esther would have thought such a claim impossible, but now her eyes were open, she understood that time was an element like any other. It was as fluid as water, as gritty as sand. But still, the idea that she could really have been born so many years ago was extraordinary.

'No,' she said. 'I don't believe it.'

'Belief is for Christians,' said the cat. 'For us, only the unimaginable is impossible. I sent you away to protect you and I sent the book with you to protect our ways. Conjury was at an end so I wrote the book and sent it with you so that it may be reborn again one day.'

'But I didn't have the book. Ringmore had it.'

'Ringmore was sold the book by a man whose shop had burnt down. It was a shop to which the nuns frequently sold items that had been left with the orphans in their care. They sold your birthright for a couple of pennies and denied that which should have been yours. I've been trying to guide it back into your hands ever since.'

'Why should I believe any of this?' said Esther. 'What do you want from me?'

'I want to be a friend to you.'

'Leave me alone.' Esther angrily swung her staff at the cat. It jumped off the wall to avoid being hit. 'I don't want to hear your stories,' she exclaimed.

'They are the truth,' said Olwyn. 'Ask the prioress at the orphanage, then look inside yourself and you'll know that I only want to help you.'

50

Backstage

As far as Harry Clay was concerned, there were few walks as pleasurable as that from the stage to the dressing room, with the thunderous applause still ringing in his ears. The opening show had been a resounding success and yet Clay was not as happy as he should have been. He could not rid his head of the heckles during The Resurrection. This trick involved him being buried alive in a glass container, with volunteers from the audience spading on the soil themselves. However, after dramatically clawing his way out of the soil, several voices cried out that they had seen the hinge at the back of the glass cabinet. What alarmed Clay was that they were entirely correct. A small door allowed Clay to crawl out of the cabinet without spilling any tell-tale signs of dirt on the stage. The dissenters had been shouted down by other audience members and the rest of the evening had gone smoothly, but Clay still felt rattled by the experience. With so many other illusionists and escapologists working the theatres of London, it was madness to consider dropping one of his best tricks but the hecklers had compounded what he already knew. The Remarkable Harry Clay needed something more remarkable.

'Good show tonight.' Fred handed him a towel.

'Lively crowd,' responded Clay, using it to dry the sweat from his face.

'Now, don't go dwelling on that heckling,' said Fred, adopting his serious tone. 'It was nothing, and everyone else was on your side. It was probably one of your rivals, trying to stir things up.'

'It was you who shouted him down, wasn't it?' Clay already knew the answer.

'What does it matter if it was? As soon as I rallied them, the whole crowd were with you.'

Clay removed his shirt, hurled it into a laundry basket and threw the towel over his shoulders.

'What do you think of my act? Honestly now, Fred?'

'Honestly?' replied Fred. 'I think you're the best thing on in the West End. I prefer the dancing girls, you know, but that aside . . .'

'I mean, really honestly.'

'Well, I guess you could do with a little tightening up here and there,' admitted his old friend. 'It'll happen naturally as you go through the run.'

'It's not enough. I need a new trick.'

'The whole show is new.'

'Something different then.'

Fred considered this. 'Maybe you should think about

incorporating some modern equipment into the act. Vats and closets are all very well but what about something like that motorised car you saw demonstrated the other day?'

'A motorised car? Incorporate it how?'

'I don't know. You're trapped in it as it's heading towards a cliff's edge then you jump out at the last minute . . . you know, the sort of thing you normally do?'

'The sort of thing I normally do,' Clay repeated flatly.

'I ain't knocking it. It's kept us well enough all these years.'

Fred had known Clay long enough to understand that there was no point reminding him that he was at the beginning of the longest-ever run of a one-man show in London. Nor was it worth mentioning that they were on course to sell out every night and break the theatre's box-office records. Clay's moods were Clay's moods. 'I'll get the cab to wait by the stage door,' said Fred, closing the door behind him.

Clay slumped down in his chair and stared at his own reflection, wondering how much longer he could do this, when there was a knock at the door.

'I'm still here,' he called, assuming Fred had forgotten to mention something.

In the mirror he saw the door open and two boys step inside. Behind them were two more, unable to get into the small room. He recognised them as the bunch he'd seen caught up in Esther's mud tornado. Clay placed the towel down on the counter and, using it as a cover, discreetly picked up a nail file. It wasn't much but it was the sharpest thing to hand.

'Can I help you?' he said.

'You Harry Clay?' asked Hardy.

'I was when I walked off that stage five minutes ago.'

'Do something remarkable then,' said the other boy in the room. He was younger, with dirty blond hair and shallow blue eyes.

'Yeah, do something magic,' said Hardy.

'How about a spot of mind-reading?' Clay turned to face him, still clutching the nail file under the towel. 'Now, let's see.' He raised his left hand to his temple and narrowed his eyes. 'Name. I'm getting a strong name, a tough name . . . H . . . H . . . Hard . . . Hardly . . . No. Hardy.'

Hardy slowly clapped. 'Very clever. Now my turn. You're a man with something to hide.' He whisked off the towel to reveal Clay's right hand, clutching the nail file. 'What you going to do with that then?'

Clay attempted to stand up but Brewer pushed him back into his seat and held his knife up to Clay's throat.

'Easy now, boys,' said Clay.

'Brewer's mind ain't so easy to read, is it?' said Hardy. 'That's on account of it not being so big and all. So let's stick with me. What am I thinking now?'

'You mean apart from the sadistic pleasure you're getting from all this?' said Clay.

'Yeah, apart from that.'

'It's about the book,' said Clay. 'And the orphans.'

Hardy nodded. 'First, they get the coppers after them, then there was whatever happened on the beach. I reckon you're the man to give us some answers, Harry Clay.'

'And you thought it best to come down and threaten me in order to get them?' said Clay.

'Shall I cut him?' asked Brewer. 'Show him we mean business.'

'Oh, I have no doubt that you mean business,' said Clay. 'And cutting me isn't going to get you anywhere.'

Brewer looked at Hardy, who gave him the signal to back off.

'I know you,' said Clay. 'I know your type. I could have been like you but I decided to make something of my life.'

'He thinks he's better than us,' said Brewer.

'Of course I'm better than you,' said Clay. 'Don't you want to be better than you? Look at you. Threatening and stealing. Where do you think this ends? Always the same place. At the end of a rope. That's where.'

'So what?' said Hardy. 'We can't all make rabbits appear out of hats.'

Clay touched the point in his neck where the knife had been pressed. He examined his finger and saw a spot of blood where the blade had pierced his skin. He sucked the blood off and looked at Brewer. 'How old are you?'

'What's it to you?' he replied.

'How old?'

'I'll be fourteen in May. Why?'

'And you grew up in the same orphanage as the others?'

Brewer raised his knife again. 'What's this about?'

Clay smiled. 'How would you feel if I were to offer you an opportunity to make some money? How would you feel if I offered you a way out?'

Brewer glanced at Hardy.

'What kind of money?' asked Hardy.

'Real money,' said Clay. 'Money you couldn't even dream of.'

'We're listening,' said Hardy, 'but I'm warning you now: try and get one over on me and my boys, and you'll find yourself in a situation you won't be escaping from so easily.'

51

Vulnerability

Sitting up a tree in Brunswick Square, Tom was amusing himself by manipulating one of the tree branches and using it to pluck the purses, wallets and handkerchiefs from pockets of passers-by.

'Is this really what you choose to do with your power?' said Mondriat, landing on the branch beside him.

'I can do what I want,' replied Tom, sulkily.

'And I want to help you do that.'

'Why? Why did you make me do the Creation Spell?' said Tom. 'Why do you want to be my familiar? What do you want?'

'I only want to witness –' began Mondriat.

'Yes, I know. You want to witness the beauty of Conjury. Whatever you say. I still don't trust you.'

'Quite right. Trust is folly.'

'So you're saying I'm right not to trust you?'

'You should never let anyone have your complete trust,

but I promise I mean you no harm, Tom.'

'Prove it,' said Tom.

'How can I prove it?'

'Show me your face, your human face. Take me to your mirror.'

Mondriat flapped his wings and hopped agitatedly up and down. 'You would have me make myself vulnerable to you?'

'Yes. Show me it and I'll know that you trust me and so I'll trust you.'

'Oh, very well,' said the magpie. 'If that is what it will take, come on.'

Mondriat fluttered to the ground. Tom jumped down after him and followed the bird through the square, his new black cloak billowing behind him.

'Quite the Conjuror you look too,' sniggered Mondriat.

Tom ignored him. He liked it. It matched his black stick. He had visited a tailor after splitting with Esther. It hadn't taken much effort to persuade him to make a black cloak for him. Tom enjoyed the way it moved as he walked and the way it made him feel larger when it caught the wind.

Mondriat led him to the British Museum, a splendid old building. The old Tom would have been intimidated by such a place, but the new Tom merely considered how he could have reduced it to dust with the wave of his hand if he so desired.

'The doormen are not overly keen on allowing birds in, so if you wouldn't mind making us both invisible,' said Mondriat.

Mondriat hopped onto his shoulder. Tom moved his staff then swished his cloak around him and vanished from sight.

'Very stylishly done,' said Mondriat. 'Inside now, please.'

Tom followed an elderly couple inside. 'Up there,' said Mondriat.

Tom walked up the grand staircase, until Mondriat told him to stop in front of a grand mirror.

'This is it?' asked Tom.

'You tell me,' said Mondriat.

Tom wafted away the invisibility spell and watched as his reflection reappeared in the mirror. Mondriat was on his shoulder but the mirror showed a man standing beside him. He turned to look at Mondriat then back at his reflection. He had brown hair, a well-trimmed beard, hazel eyes and a wide smile.

'This is what you looked like?' said Tom.

'I know. A handsome devil.'

'This was always your mirror?'

'My father made it,' said Mondriat. 'He was a Venetian mirror-maker. He made this one just before he died. Beautiful, isn't it? It became a part of the collection donated to this museum.'

'So how does it work?' asked Tom. 'How would I steal your Conjury?'

The fear was evident in Mondriat's reflected face. 'Now, why would you want to know such a thing?'

'What's the matter? You don't trust me?' said Tom.

'Can I, Tom? Can I trust you?' asked Mondriat.

'That's why it's called trust,' said Tom. 'You don't know.'

Mondriat sighed. 'Smashing the mirror would kill me, but you would lose the power. To draw it out you need to hold a second mirror opposite this one. You could coax the True Reflection out and intercept it as it moved.' He looked nervously at Tom. 'Is that what you want to do?'

'Maybe,' said Tom. 'Certainly, if you get on my nerves.'

'But not now,' said Mondriat.

'Not yet,' said Tom.

'So we must trust each other. Now, please let me help you.'

'Help me do what?'

'Help you achieve everything you desire. Wealth, power, strength. This is what you seek. It is what everyone seeks. I can help you find the power to shape your own destiny.'

'How?' asked Tom.

'A Conjuror manipulates. He does not create. To achieve your goals you will need powerful allies. You will need to find those who can exchange your gifts for theirs.'

'I'm listening.'

'Good, then you can stop this pickpocketing tree nonsense. You need to stay out of sight. You must be as invisible as the air. Get rid of this cape while you're at it. Try to blend in rather than stand out.'

'I'll do what you say,' said Tom. 'But I'm keeping the cape.'

52

Eternity

Lord Ringmore was philosophical about the failure of the experiment with Sir Tyrrell's nephew. After all, the creation of a new Conjuror would only have further complicated matters. The goal was to entice the orphans back into his employment and, with Clay's new stage show, Hayman's novel and Sir Tyrrell's parliamentary work keeping the rest of them busy, it was down to him alone to achieve it. There was every possibility that the orphans had left London, but Lord Ringmore had a feeling that this was not the case. Tom and Esther had grown up in these streets. It was all they knew. Still, London was a large enough city to get lost in, even without the ability to turn invisible.

Sir Tyrrell had furnished Lord Ringmore with a letter of introduction to the metropolitan police, giving him unrestricted access to the Central London Police Station on Agar Street. It was whilst there that he caught wind of a number of reports about a pickpocket operating in Brunswick Square.

Nothing strange in that, of course, except that some of the accounts appeared to suggest that the criminal responsible was invisible, while others claimed that it was the large weeping willow in the centre of the square that was plucking items with its branches. The duty officer found the whole thing most amusing, but Lord Ringmore had immediately caught a hansom cab there.

Taking a leaf out of Clay's book, Lord Ringmore had left his top hat, cape and walking stick at home, instead dressing in an anonymous dirt-brown overcoat with a cap pulled down to cover his face. In this disguise, he stood watching the square until he saw a boy drop out of a tree. It was Tom, even if his black cape and walking stick made Lord Ringmore feel as though he was looking at a miniature version of himself.

When the boy vanished from sight outside the British Library, Lord Ringmore's heart pounded. Having spent his life circumnavigating the globe in search of magic, here it was in his home city: real magic. When Tom reappeared he knew he could not risk losing him again so he stepped out in front of the boy and spoke. 'Hello, Tom.'

'What do you want?' replied the orphan.

'To strike up a deal.'

On Tom's shoulder was a disgustingly mangy magpie, which squawked in a most peculiar manner. It seemed to Lord Ringmore that the boy was listening to its unintelligible utterances.

Tom looked at Lord Ringmore. 'All right,' he said. 'But not like last time. I got more to bargain with now.'

'You most certainly have,' acknowledged Lord Ringmore.

He paid for a cab to transport all three of them to his house, where he led the boy and his strange, feathered companion inside. When Tom looked around the room, empty but for a single armchair, he said, 'Don't expect me to say sorry.'

'I expect no apologies,' said Lord Ringmore. 'I daresay my possessions are worth a great deal more to whoever now holds them than they ever meant to me.'

'What you thinking anyway, leaving a big house like this with no one home?' asked Tom. 'You should have a house-keeper to watch the place when you're not in. Or a dog. Or something.'

'I accept full culpability,' said Lord Ringmore.

'You got the book though, did you?' said Tom.

Lord Ringmore nodded.

'You know I could take it back if I wanted,' said Tom.

Another movement from Tom's staff and Lord Ringmore felt the book wrestle itself free of his inside pocket and fly across the room into the boy's hand. Lord Ringmore tapped the spot where the book had been. His heart was pounding harder than a military drummer. 'How does it feel?' he asked. 'I mean, to possess such power at your fingertips?'

'You already know how it feels.' Tom shrugged. 'Since I can remember, I've been told what to do, where to go, how to feel. Now, I can choose for myself. So don't ask me how it feels as though you can't imagine it because you've known that feeling your whole life.'

'And what do you want now?' asked Lord Ringmore.

'I want my share.'

'Your share of what?'

'Of everything.'

Lord Ringmore picked up a glass of wine from the mantelpiece. 'You mean, you want money?'

'Yeah money, of course money, but I want to be someone too.'

Lord Ringmore took a sip of wine. 'Oh, I think we can arrange that easily enough,' he said. 'After all, you're more someone than anyone I've ever met. But, tell me, can you not magic up everything you desire?'

'Conjurers can only manipulate,' said Tom. 'It is the unInfected like you who make.'

'Then we can do great things together, you and I, Tom,' said Lord Ringmore. 'You will have money, means and everything you desire, but I also have one request.'

'Which is what?' asked Tom.

'Oh, only eternity,' said Lord Ringmore, casually. 'Only eternity.'

53

Lesson

The main door of St Clement's Catholic School for Waifs and Strays was kept locked and bolted at all times, keeping the orphans inside and everyone else out. As far as Mother Agnes was concerned, the large bolted door was essential to keep out the snakes of temptation that slithered through the city, but the locks yielded easily as Esther waved her hand, and she stepped inside. Tom used to joke that he would only ever come back when he was wealthy enough to buy the place. He would turn the nuns out into the street, make them strip and shave their heads, just as Mother Agnes had done to the orphans every time there was the threat of head lice. They had stood, shivering as the sleet came down on their frozen bodies, while they waited to have their heads shaved.

Esther was not back for revenge. She was there because she wanted the truth.

Walking down the corridor Esther could hear the chanting

from the classroom. '*Two times two is four . . . three times two is six . . . four times two is eight . . .*' She looked in at the rows of orphans, terrified of making a mistake or being caught miming, knowing that to do so would be to incur severe punishment.

A girl called Naomi spotted Esther at the window. A few years younger than Esther, she had always looked up to her. Esther recalled the time Naomi had claimed God was speaking to her at night. Esther had begged her not to tell anyone but word got out and, when it reached Mother Agnes, she had dragged Naomi in front of the school and explained that it was not the voice of God she was hearing. It was that of Satan.

This memory came back to Esther as Naomi spied her through the classroom window and waved excitedly. It wasn't long before the other orphans noticed. When Mother Agnes saw the class's attention slip she did not turn to see what they were looking at but instead charged across the room with her ruler raised. Esther quickly sent the ruler flying in the air, then clattering to the floor. Mother Agnes spun around in confusion and saw Esther step inside.

'You are no longer welcome in this charitable institution!' said Mother Agnes accusingly. 'After all I have done for you . . .'

'What did you do?' demanded Esther.

'You are a child.' Mother Agnes spat the words. 'You do not understand the sacrifices we make here for you. Daily sacrifices. Your very existence is testament to the Christian kindness of this charitable institution, without which you would be dead in the street.'

'Yes, I am a miracle,' said Esther.

'You insolent child –'

With the slightest of movements, Esther killed the words in her throat. 'The beatings, the cruelties, the nights sent to bed hungry for no good reason,' she said. 'This is what you did for me.'

'We take those whose parents cannot care for them and bring them up as God would have us do,' said Mother Agnes.

'Would God have you beat children?' said Esther. 'Does God make you punish those whose only sin is to be hungry? No God I know would do that.'

'No, I can see perfectly well that you have allowed another to be your master,' hissed Mother Agnes.

'Not him, neither,' said Esther.

Mother Agnes picked up her ruler and raised her hand. 'With these children as my witness I will beat the devil from you, child.' Mother Agnes swung the ruler, but Esther sent it into the nun's unsuspecting face. The sound of wood against skin echoed off the walls and the children stared in awe.

'Behold, this child of Satan,' cried Mother Agnes, as her cheek reddened. 'She wields his terrible power as he claws at her insides. This is what will happen to you if you sell your soul, as this poor wretch has done. Look upon the face of evil.'

'Yes, look upon the face of evil,' repeated Esther.

'I should have left you to die, along with your mother,' said the prioress.

'What do you know about her?'

'Only that I found you clinging to her dead body, child. I lifted you off her cold breast myself. I buried your mother in a pauper's grave and took you in.'

Esther didn't need to perform a spell to recognise this as the truth. 'What else was there?'

'Nothing else.'

'Liar. There was a book.'

'It was a long time ago,' replied Mother Agnes. 'Orphans are left with all sorts of things, but their lives begin afresh here.'

'What happened to it?'

'Any items left with children are sold to help pay for their upbringing. Not that your book fetched much. It was as worthless as was your mother's life.'

'It was mine,' said Esther firmly.

'There is only one book you should concern yourself with. The Bible. It's a good thing your mother is dead. No mother would want to live to see her child dwell so readily with Lucifer.'

Esther would have sent the ruler flying into her old enemy's face again but she was scared that if she allowed herself to give in to this small temptation, she would not be able to stop. Instead, she placed her left hand on Mother Agnes's cheek, while moving the staff with her right hand. Mother Agnes was unable to move away. Her eyes were closed and yet she could not avoid seeing that which Esther had to show her. Esther projected the images in her mind. She showed her the truth she had learnt. She showed Mother

Agnes that the world was not as she believed. It was so much deeper, stranger, darker and lighter. She felt the prioress try to look away as she forced her to witness the true nature of the universe. As Tom had destroyed his aunt's house, so Esther would do the same to Mother Agnes's mind. Piece by piece, she tore her faith to shreds. Mother Agnes tried to hide from the onslaught, but the further she ran into her mind, the more she revealed of herself and the quicker Esther could pollute her every thought with crippling doubt.

When Esther removed her hand, Mother Agnes opened her eyes and collapsed to the floor in tears. The orphans stared in wonder as the nun they feared more than any other clasped her hands together and muttered under her breath, 'Forgive me . . . forgive me', as though in prayer. Only Esther knew that she was not praying. Prayer was no longer an option for Mother Agnes. Esther had robbed her of her faith.

54

Wasteland

Clay led Hardy and his boys to a patch of wasteland where the only signs of life came from the boat-dwelling gypsies moored nearby. The sound of strumming guitars, hand clapping and laughter drifted through the cold night air.

'What's out here?' asked Hardy.

'Nothing,' replied Clay. 'That's the point. No one can see us out here.'

'I don't like being so near all them gypsies,' said Worms.

'Nor me,' said Stump.

'They won't bother us if we don't bother them,' said Clay. 'Now, you'll need a stick.'

'Why?' asked Brewer.

'To act as your wand,' replied Clay.

'Is he gonna turn us into toads or something?' said Worms, making Stump snigger.

'Not a lot of turning required for that,' said Hardy. 'Now, shut it.'

'This is stupid,' grumbled Brewer.

'You all saw what Esther did,' said Hardy. 'I want to know how.'

'What if I don't want to?' said Brewer.

Hardy grabbed him in a headlock and banged his head with his knuckles. 'You do what I say when you're in my gang. You know that, Brewer.'

'Here. What about this one?' said Clay, offering a branch he had found.

Brewer took it and snapped it on his knee. 'It's rotten,' he said.

'Try this.' Hardy held out the ruler he had taken from Mother Agnes.

'*Quiet reflection*,' said Brewer, taking it gently in both hands.

'Thought you might remember it,' said Hardy. 'You must have felt it almost as many times as I did.'

'So what now?' asked Brewer. He waved it in the air. Worms and Stump laughed loudly. Across the way, on the boats, the music stopped.

'Quiet,' whispered Hardy. 'You don't want to find yourselves in the middle of a gypsy brawl.'

The guitar started playing again.

'Draw this shape on the ground.' Clay held up a piece of paper. 'Draw it big enough for you to stand in the middle circle.'

Brewer looked at it doubtfully.

'Come on, Brewer, draw the shape,' said Hardy.

Brewer took the piece of paper, stared at it then copied

it out onto the ground with his stick.

'Now, step into the centre,' said Clay.

'What is this? Piggy in the middle?' asked Worms.

'Do it, Brewer,' ordered Hardy.

As soon as Brewer stepped into the circle, to the others' surprise he began to shake as though he was experiencing some kind of fit.

'What's happening?' demanded Hardy.

'I don't know,' said Clay.

'Brewer, what are you feeling?' asked Hardy.

Brewer stepped out of the circle and turned to face Hardy.

'Brewer?' Hardy stepped back uncertainly.

Brewer gazed at the ruler in his hand, his eyes glowing strangely.

'I feel . . .' He searched for the right word. 'I feel . . . strong.'

'We should get moving,' said Clay. The guitar had stopped again and the gypsies were shouting and moving towards them.

'Good strong?' asked Hardy.

'Good for *me*,' replied Brewer. He crouched down and moved the ruler in his right hand. He held his left up to Hardy's chest, throwing him onto his back.

'Why you . . .' Hardy jumped up, but this time Brewer sent him flying over his head.

The gypsies were closing in, with flaming torches in their hands.

'I think we should all get out of here,' said Clay.

'Why?' asked Brewer.

He clenched his fist and the flames from the gypsies' torches shot into the air. The fire formed monstrous faces with a snake-like body that swung down to earth. Hardy tried to run, but Brewer clicked his fingers and brought him tumbling down again, manipulating him like a puppet. The gypsies had dropped their torches and were running scared, but the fire-creature moved in on Hardy.

'Come on, Brewer, we're friends, ain't we?' he shouted, desperately trying to escape the flaming beast that was crawling towards him.

'It was always going to come to this,' said Brewer.

'Come on, Brewer, we've all had a good laugh,' said Worms.

'Yeah, leave him alone now,' added Stump.

'He deserves this,' snarled Brewer, and he slammed his ruler on the ground. The fire-beast opened its mouth wide and pounced on Hardy. The others looked away as the flames devoured him until his desperate screams were silenced.

Brewer lowered his hand.

'We need to leave now,' said Clay, urgently.

'You're right,' said Brewer. 'There's nothing left here I care about.'

They turned and fled, leaving behind them the burnt cinders of Hardy's dead body.

55

Perfection

Ever since being stuck inside these birds' bodies Mondriat had hated waking up. In his dreams he was still a powerful, handsome Conjuror, rather than a rotten old magpie. This time, when he awoke he opened his eyes to find a huge, black, feline face looming over him.

'Olwyn,' he said, groggily. 'Don't do that! You want me to die of terror?'

'Of terror? Of course not,' she replied. 'Dreaming of me, were you, Mondriat?'

'Always.'

'I understand you have directed the boy back into Ringmore's hands. Why? What are you up to, Mondriat?'

'Tom needed an ally. He needed someone able to give him what he wants.'

Olwyn licked a paw and used it to clean her face. 'And what does the Lord want in return?' she asked.

'Ah, yes, well. Interesting you should ask that. He's rather got his sights set on immortality.' Mondriat chuckled.

'How do you expect to deliver that?'

'Oh you know, I thought Tom could come up with something that makes him feel immortal. After all, one doesn't really know that one isn't immortal until it's too late, does one?'

Olwyn prowled forward and Mondriat stepped back nervously. 'How would you feel if I could tell you that it is possible?' Olwyn's green eyes twinkled playfully.

'What do you mean?' Mondriat asked warily.

'Ringmore wants immortality. He's gone to the boy for answers but he already has the solution in his possession.'

'He does?' Mondriat was struggling to keep up.

'Haven't you worked it out yet?' Olwyn sighed.

'The book. You're talking about the book?' said Mondriat.

'Yes, the book,' she said patiently. 'You asked me what it was for. The truth is I wrote it in order to discover the Eternity Spell.'

'By writing a book?'

'For you, Conjury was instinctive. For me, it was an exact science. Through writing down every spell and every potion, I was able to study how each shape affected the power it drew. Slowly, methodically, I searched for the answer.'

Mondriat twitched his tail excitedly. 'Are you saying you worked it out?'

The cat nodded. 'Yes. The final spell in the book is the Eternity Spell.'

'But that's . . . that's remarkable. Why did you never tell me?'

'You were too busy robbing mirrors and, besides, I never trusted you.'

Mondriat wished he could read something in Olwyn's feline expression. Affection, bitterness; anything. But it was impossible. 'Why are you telling me now?' he asked.

'I had hoped the girl might perform the spell but now you have the boy and the book, it makes sense that he should draw the spell.'

'Yes, but why involve me after all this time?'

'Mondriat,' purred the cat, 'if the boy performs the Eternity Spell, he can bring us both back.'

'Back?'

Olwyn moved closer to Mondriat so that he could feel her breath on his face. 'Finally, my love,' she whispered in his ear. 'Finally, we can return to human form.'

'Is it possible?'

'Yes. Imagine it, Mondriat. You and I, human once again. Conjuror and Conjuress again.'

Mondriat felt his magpie heart speed up to such an extent that it reminded him it really was about time he found a new body, but if this was all true then that new body would be his own, human self.

'Oh Olwyn, you wondrous woman,' he proclaimed. He wanted to kiss her but realised that it would be as impractical as it was inadvisable. Instead he hopped up and down and flapped his wings. 'This is marvellous . . . marvellous,' he said. Then a thought struck him. 'But if you succeeded in finding the Eternity Spell back then, how did you end up like this?'

'There were complications,' she replied. 'But this time we will get it right. Now, let me explain what your boy needs to do.'

56

Demonstration

When Georgina Waters had first stepped off the boat from New York to England, she had felt as though she could actually smell the magic of this old country, lingering in the dense fog. England's rich history was there in the brickwork of the buildings, the names of the towns and the pale faces of its weather-beaten people.

As time had passed and Georgina Waters became Mr G. Hayman, her interest in magic had not diminished, but she had started to wonder if the stories of old weren't better suited to her works of fiction than to anything remotely real. She had heard so much about the old ways, but had never witnessed them for herself.

The discovery of the book had reinvigorated her faith. Joining Sir Tyrrell and Lord Ringmore in his sparsely furnished drawing room, she commented on Harry Clay's absence.

'He sent word that he is too occupied with his theatre

show to attend this evening's meeting,' replied Lord Ringmore. 'More fool him, for tonight we have a special guest. The Society of Thirteen has recruited a new member.'

'You have found an appropriately aged orphan?' asked Sir Tyrrell.

'A birth certificate might be worth asking for this time,' said Mr G. Hayman.

'That won't be necessary. Will it, Tom?'

In the centre of the room a boy materialised. He was dressed in a cloak and held a staff in one hand. On his shoulder was a magpie. Mr G. Hayman and Sir Tyrrell stared, open mouthed.

'May I introduce our newest member?' announced Lord Ringmore, evidently enjoying the reaction.

Mr G. Hayman reached a hand to touch Tom's arm and confirm that her eyes were not fooling her other senses but he moved it away and stared defiantly at her.

'I'm sorry,' she said. 'It's just . . . I have waited so long.'

'We all have,' said Lord Ringmore.

'Forgive me,' said Sir Tyrrell. 'But I have seen many wondrous things and many remarkable fakes. How do we know the boy is genuine?'

Tom raised his left hand and beckoned Lord Ringmore's hat from his head. It floated across the room into his hand. He showed it to the others, revealing that it was empty. 'What would you have me pull out of this hat to make you believe?' he said. 'A rabbit? A treasured object of yours?' He pushed his arm into the hat, much further than should have been possible. 'Or perhaps something of greater value to you.' As he reached deep into the hat, Sir Tyrrell suddenly clutched his chest. He grew short of breath and stared in disbelief at Tom.

'You feel that, do you?' asked Tom. 'You see, if I wanted to I could pull out your beating heart. Would that be proof enough for you? If I wanted I could draw the air from your lungs or drain the blood from your veins.'

Sir Tyrrell gasped for breath.

'Enough, Tom,' said Lord Ringmore.

Tom unclenched his hand and Sir Tyrrell took a deep breath as the pain vanished from his chest.

'I ain't no stage magician,' said Tom. 'I'm a Conjuror. I can do anything I can imagine.' He handed the hat back to Lord Ringmore.

'Tom is going to help us achieve our goal,' he said, placing the hat back on his head.

'The Eternity Spell,' whispered Mr G. Hayman. 'But even Olwyn never discovered it.' She watched the magpie hop onto a mantelpiece, its long tail twitching as it followed the conversation.

'Or so we thought,' said Lord Ringmore. He held the book open at its last page, which contained the most intricately drawn shape of all. 'Olwyn Broe's final spell. The Eternity Spell.'

'Are we sure?' asked Mr G. Hayman.

The magpie clicked and flapped its wings angrily.

'Tom says his familiar has confirmed it. This is the spell.' Lord Ringmore banged his stick excitedly on the wooden floorboards.

'So are we to perform it now?' asked Sir Tyrrell.

'No,' said Tom. 'Not here. We need to find a place where the lifeblood is most powerful. We need to be close to the heart of the Earthsoul.'

'And where would that be?' asked Sir Tyrrell.

'They say the Earthsoul flows through the rivers of the world. It drives them down from the mountains. It makes the oceans breathe with its tides. It fills the veins of the world,' said Mr G. Hayman.

'So, near the Thames,' said Sir Tyrrell.

'For the spell to work we must be right in its heart,' said Tom.

Sir Tyrrell looked exasperated. 'What does all this mean?'

'We need to be under the river,' said Tom.

57

Reinvention

Fred had stuck by his old friend, Harry Clay, through some outlandish requests. He had barely batted an eyelid when Clay first asked him to chain him up and throw him into a vat of water. He had happily agreed when Clay asked him to bury him alive. He had wavered when Clay had asked him to shoot a loaded pistol at him but, when it came to it, he had put his faith in Harry, aimed and fired.

This one felt different. It wasn't the first time Harry had asked Fred to speak to the theatre management, but this was pure insanity. Clay had returned home late after the opening night, offering no explanation of where he had been, but instead ranting about finally having found it. When Fred enquired what he had found, Clay's eyes had lit up and he had responded, 'Something worth selling.'

'I thought we already had that,' replied Fred.

'Not like this. I need you to speak to Mr Dickey for me and tell him we're taking a break.'

Fred laughed at this joke but his old friend's expression suggested that he was deadly serious.

'We've only just started our run,' protested Fred.

'We're restarting . . . we're reinventing.'

'Why? The tickets are already sold.' Fred had often wondered if his friend's regular oxygen deprivation would lead to some kind of mental problems. Was this the moment that Fred would watch it all slip away?

'I want everyone refunded,' said Harry.

'Refunded?'

'Every last one of them. We need to up the price and resell the tickets. Except for the press. I want every newspaperman in London here for the new opening night. Put them in the stalls to make sure they can see every little detail.'

'Mr Dickey will never go for it.'

'I need you to make sure he does go for it. I'm relying on you, Fred.'

'I'll need to give him something to go on.'

Harry shook his head. 'Sorry.'

'Then I need something. I need to understand why you're doing this, Harry.'

Harry walked to the liquor cabinet and took a swig of the first bottle that came to hand. 'You know I would if I could but this one's got to remain a secret.'

'All this time and I never once asked you how you did any of those tricks. Not one,' said Fred. 'I never wanted to know. If I didn't know, I reckoned, then no matter who came creeping around trying to find out I wouldn't be able to tell them nothing. But asking all this, we're talking a lot of money, Harry, and not just yours, neither.'

Harry placed the bottle back on the table.

'Don't worry. We'll all be a lot richer by the end of this run. You, Dickey, me, the lot of us.'

'You're cancelling three shows and a matinée then giving half the stall tickets away free to journalists. You need arithmetic lessons.'

'We're doubling the price of the tickets.'

'*Doubling*?'

Harry reached for the bottle but Fred snatched it away. Harry stared back, sullenly. 'You've never let me down, Fred,' said Harry. 'Don't start now.'

'The same to you,' replied Fred.

'Everything I've done is nothing compared with what I'm going to unveil next week.'

Fred looked at his old friend. If this was the onset of insanity, which he strongly suspected, then it really was the beginning of the end. If so, Fred would embrace it the same way he had embraced the madness at the start.

'All right,' he said at last. 'I'll tell old Dickey. Don't blame me if we end up being thrown out and having our name so badly besmirched that we're stuck touring the provinces for the rest of our lives.'

'All I need is that new opening night,' said Clay. 'After that, the tickets will sell themselves, no matter how much I charge. Oh, and one last thing. I need a new sign outside the theatre. Twice as big, and it needs to read: The Miraculous Harry Clay brings you, for the first time ever, REAL MAGIC.'

58

History

Esther missed Tom. She wanted to talk to him and make things better, but how could she when she had let him down so badly? It didn't make it any better that she had been right about his aunt. By trying to protect him, she had only succeeded in further driving him away.

Esther stood outside Lord Ringmore's house, watching the ripples created by Tom's spells, wanting to be near him but unable to approach. He was inside, performing for the Society. Esther wondered what they were doing for him in return. What was the point in working for Lord Ringmore now that she and Tom could do anything they wanted? If the only limitation was one's own imagination then why were they still here in this grimy city, barely any better off than before?

Esther had cast a spell of invisibility around her but the tall, dark figure dressed in animal hides who stopped in front of her stared directly into her eyes.

'You may be invisible to the unInfected, but I see you,' said Kiyaya.

'Your friend could see you too, if he chose. Perhaps that is what you want.'

Esther shrugged off the spell. After everything she had learnt over the last few days, she thought nothing else could surprise her. Now it appeared that Kiyaya could not only speak English but that he was a Conjuror.

'I thought all the Infected were wiped out,' she said.

'Here, in your cold continent, yes, but where I am from, the few still roam.'

'Does Mr Symmonds know?'

'John Symmonds knew nothing, but he was a good man. He gave me transportation to England. I like it here. I can live freely here.'

'Why weren't you free where you came from?'

'In my homeland,' he said, thumping his chest, 'the Infected are not trusted, and so they are forced to walk alone.'

'Then why would you choose such a life?'

'Let me show you.'

He reached out a hand. Esther stepped back and held up her staff defensively.

'No harm will come to you,' said Kiyaya, speaking in such a calm, measured voice that Esther lowered her staff and allowed him to place his hand on her shoulder. Feeling its weight, the world went blank. When she opened her eyes, London had been replaced by a wild and rugged landscape. There were rolling hills, valleys of red rock and strange, spiky trees rising out of the dusty ground. It was like nothing she had ever seen. It was more space than she had ever imagined.

'My home,' Kiyaya's voice filled her head. 'This is one of my earliest memories.'

The eyes through which she was witnessing this vision blinked, and suddenly she was inside a tent made from brown animal skins. Inside the tent sat a man, woman and child, all dressed like Kiyaya. From the angle she was watching them, Esther realised she was seeing through the eyes of an infant.

'These are your parents?' she asked.

'No. My parents dead. This is my father's brother, his wife and their son.'

Esther heard a child's scream and the uncle turned and approached. His large face loomed over and picked up the distressed infant. The love was evident in his eyes, but his wife remained with her arms around her own child.

'They looked after me. My uncle was a kind man but his own son always came first. Kiyaya came second.'

Another blink brought darkness. They were outside again. Esther heard a howling animal in the night. The eyes were older now and stood taller. They glanced around and she felt Kiyaya's fear. He looked up and Esther saw a sky of burning stars, brighter and fuller than she had ever seen.

'What's happening?' she asked.

There was a rustling from the bushes and she saw a man emerge from behind a shrub. His body was covered with strange symbols. His eyes burned like fire as they settled on the petrified boy.

'This man found Kiyaya, thirteen years old and orphaned. He showed me my better self.'

The painted man handed a stick to Kiyaya. Esther didn't need to see the shape he drew on the ground to know what was about to happen. Once again the vision shifted and they were inside the tent. On the ground, his uncle, aunt and cousin lay unconscious. Her vision blurred with Kiyaya's tears. A hand wiped them away and she was back outside Lord Ringmore's house. The Indian removed his hand from her shoulder.

'Why are you showing me this?' she asked. 'What do you want?'

'I want to help. A time will come soon when Olwyn will need you.' Kiyaya stared unblinkingly at Esther as he said the name, searching her face for a reaction. Esther tried to give none. 'She was once a great Conjuress,' said Kiyaya. 'I believe she can help us both.'

'I don't care about her. I don't want to be a part of any of this. I want to leave all this behind.'

'And yet you remain here in this city.'

Esther said nothing.

'You will not leave because you want him to come with you, but there is much happening that you do not understand.'

'Then tell me,' demanded Esther.

'Soon I will show you,' replied Kiyaya, before turning and walking away, leaving Esther staring after him, bewildered.

59

Identification

A Catholic upbringing had left Chief Inspector Longdale with a profound mistrust of nuns. In his experience, these strange wimpled creatures could give the lowest form of criminals a run for their money when it came to the use of violence and intimidation. So far Mother Agnes had done nothing to dissuade Longdale from his firmly held belief. She stood in the mortuary, wearing a thin-lipped smile on her face in spite of the fact that there lay before her the burnt corpse of a boy.

'Well?' said Longdale, impatiently. 'Do you recognise him?'

'Yes, it's Ezekiel. I always told him he was destined to burn.'

As a copper, Longdale was used to some very black humour in the face of horror, but he shivered at the cold delivery of the joke. 'The boy's name was Hardy,' he said.

'A name he gave himself,' replied Mother Agnes. 'Each

and every child who enters our charitable institution is gifted with a good Christian name.'

'He was found on the south bank of the Thames at Battersea. Any idea what one of your boys would have been doing there?'

'He was no longer one of my boys. He made his choice to leave our protection. After they have done that, there is little we can do for them. Lucifer employs them for his ends.'

'There is bruising beneath the burns,' said Longdale. 'Was he known as a scrapper in the orphanage?'

'Such activities are strictly forbidden in our charitable institution.'

'And yet so many who leave your charitable institution end up on this slab.' Longdale covered the boy's face with the sheet, no longer wanting to see the brutality of the injuries.

Mother Agnes's nostrils flared. Longdale flinched, fearing that she might actually hit him and unsure what his reaction would be if she did.

'I do not appreciate the implication of what you are saying,' she said.

'I appreciate it no more myself,' said the Chief Inspector. 'But the fact is that this is not the first boy to have left St Clement's and found himself on the wrong side of the law. Your charitable institution, as you insist on calling it, is a breeding ground for young criminals.'

'The temptations of Satan –'

'Are indeed strong, but what is it, I ask myself, that makes so many of your students susceptible to his influence? What happens within those walls that makes them so accepting of violence and fear? What do you teach these children?'

'These are not children,' snapped Mother Agnes. 'The animal that lies on your slab is the devil's own spawn.'

'What about his cohorts?' Longdale checked his list of names. 'Brewer, Stump and Worms.'

'None of them names I recognise.'

'And yet when they find themselves here in the mortuary I fear you will recognise the faces.'

Mother Agnes stared back at him angrily. 'What do you want from me, Chief Inspector? You want me to tell you that the Lord has abandoned us? That hell is risen and is all around us? You want to hear the truth that despair is all that we have left now?'

'I seek the reason behind this boy's untimely death.'

'And you think I can help you with that?'

'Did he ever come back to the orphanage?'

'We do not have time for visits from those who have turned their backs on us.'

'Quite the Christian attitude, I'm sure.'

'We can only forgive those who seek forgiveness. The unrepentant are damned.'

'And yet as a representative of the law I must treat all as equals.'

For a moment, nun and policeman stood in deadlock, but with his steely glare Longdale made it quite clear that Mother Agnes was not leaving until she had told him what he needed to know.

'He did come back,' she admitted, finally. 'There was

something between him and some other ex-pupils, Tom and Esther. He was looking for them. I don't know why. He threatened me and stole from me.'

'What did you tell him?'

'That another had come with the same intention, a man by the name of Harry Clay.'

'The illusionist?'

'Yes, I believe that is what you would call him. Now, if we're quite finished here I'd like to return to the school.'

Chief Inspector Longdale stepped out of the nun's way. 'By all means,' he said. 'But I will be keeping a close eye on your donations to this mortuary. As I said before. No one is above the law, Mother Agnes. No one.'

60

Miraculous

As predicted, the manager of the Theatre Royal, Mr Dickey, was not impressed with Clay's sudden change of heart. Not impressed at all. At first he thought it a clumsy attempt to blackmail him into giving up a larger cut of the profits but, whether through Fred's persuasive nature or Harry's ability to draw crowds, Mr Dickey finally agreed to all of Clay's demands. Fred was expecting a little gratitude for his efforts but Harry was busy with his preparations and barely registered the news when he told him.

Clay was spending most of his time in secret rehearsals and Fred was worried about the company he was keeping. He seemed inseparable at the moment from three juveniles that Fred had never seen before, but instantly knew were trouble. He wondered if the three boys had something on Clay that bound him to them, but when he brought up that subject, Clay dismissed it entirely.

Finally, when the new opening night came, Fred watched

the drastically reduced audience arrive at the theatre. He went to wish his old friend good luck, only to be stopped by Stump and Worms, standing guard at the entrance to the backstage area. When they refused to let him pass Fred did not hold back in letting them know exactly what he thought about them. 'I've known Harry since before you were born,' he said, after letting loose with a tirade of abuse.

'No one's to pass,' said Worms.

'Not a soul,' agreed Stump.

Fred let rip with more colourfully worded insults until Clay arrived to see what the fuss was about.

'I'm sorry, Fred,' he said, taking him to one side. 'But I can't have anyone back here. Not even my dearest and oldest friend. You understand, don't you?'

'I don't like the company you're keeping these days.'

'A necessary evil, is all,' said Clay.

'Interesting choice of words.'

'Fred, we've known kids like this all our lives. We grew up around them. I can control them because I know what they want. But please, I need you to keep the faith, Fred. Stand at the back and gauge what reaction I get.'

'Harry, you know I love you but you had better pull this one off. Otherwise we're done, you and me.'

'When you see tonight's performance you'll forget all this. Just wait and see.'

Fred found an inconspicuous spot at the back, where he could hear the grumbles of those who had bothered to fork out twice the original ticket price. The journalists, with their free entry, were no better disposed towards Harry

Clay. It was going to take a spectacular performance to prevent them from writing obituaries, mourning the death of his career.

'Miraculous,' snorted a Fleet-Street man with a nose like a pig.

'Water into wine won't be enough for this crowd,' replied another with the complexion of a tomato. 'This lot are baying for blood.'

'Good line. You going to use that or can I have it?' replied the other.

Nor did the audience's antagonism diminish when the curtain went up. Clay stepped onto the stage to the sound of jeers and boos.

'Ladies and gentlemen,' he began, once they had died down. 'You know me as a master of illusion. Tonight I stand before you to tell you that everything I have done, everything I have achieved up to this point has been mere deception. Exceptionally executed deception of course but, none the less, no more impressive than the man who stands on the corner of Oxford Street, asking you to find the coin from the three available cups.'

'Harry Clay confesses all,' cried the pig-nosed journalist.

Clay continued, unshaken. 'But tonight I say goodbye to the remarkable and offer up the utterly inexplicable.'

'Not to mention the outrageously priced,' cried a voice from the circle.

'You can have your money back if you are not completely satisfied,' said Clay. 'You see, I have recently learnt that there are forces in this world that are not visible to our mortal eyes.'

'Has Harry Clay converted to spiritualism then?' asked the red-faced journalist.

'These last few days my eyes have been opened,' said Clay. 'I beg that you keep yours open too. Please, everyone, watch carefully.'

Clay clapped his hands together and, with the entire audience as his witness, vanished into thin air. There was no puff of smoke or well-placed screen to hide the trick. It was so astonishing that the audience seemed unsure how to react.

'Trapdoor, Clay?' cried someone.

'I paid double the price for this?' shouted another. 'I want my money back.'

The dissenting voices grew into a crescendo of abuse. Fred was wondering whether he should leave now and avoid another encounter with Mr Dickey when the voices died away. Everyone was looking up, wide eyed and open mouthed. Fred stepped forward and saw the reason. Clay was floating down through the auditorium, arms outstretched. He landed in the centre aisle and those in the seats nearby leapt up and clamoured to feel for the invisible wires. Desperate to understand and explain the trick, more and more pushed themselves towards him until Harry was lost beneath a scrum of people.

'Oi, back off,' shouted Fred.

Then, suddenly, the clawing mob was thrown off and Harry Clay emerged, his body entirely surrounded by huge yellow flames. It was beautiful to look at, angelic in its splendour and unlike anything anyone had ever seen. Harry grinned, then performed an impossibly graceful backwards somersault and landed back on the stage.

Finally, the applause came. The half-full auditorium produced the loudest noise Fred had ever heard. It was the reaction Harry Clay had searched for his whole life. It was beyond appreciation. As the audience took to its feet, Fred wondered whether Jesus Christ had received such applause at the wedding at Cana.

There was only one moment when something went wrong. Later in the act, Clay asked members of the audience to hold up personal items. Then, without taking one step off the stage, he managed to pluck a selection of these and draw them through the air into his own hand. One of these items was the pig-nosed journalist's pen. Clay beckoned it easily enough but when he attempted to send it back, he found it would not go. Making up some excuse about the unpredictability of magic, Clay attempted to walk it back but found his feet now glued to the ground. He tried to throw the pen but it would not leave his hand. Clay tried to hide his annoyance and make out that it was all part of the act but Fred could see the frustration on his old friend's face.

'Enough,' cried Clay at last, and the pen finally floated back to its owner to the sound of yet more applause.

61

Nero

Sir Tyrrell had pulled a lot of strings to obtain private access to the railway tunnel that ran between Rotherhithe and Wapping. The night watchman at Rotherhithe Station had considered it most irregular but he had been easily silenced with a sizable bank note and the promise of a night off. The Society of Thirteen had the tunnel to themselves.

At the centre of the tunnel, where it was widest, Tom was casting strange shadows on the curved ceiling as he performed his chaotic dance between the tracks, dragging his staff on the ground, drawing the complex spell. By his side, the magpie was perched on the open book, speaking to the boy in a language only the boy could understand. Lord Ringmore stood nearby, silently watching Tom's every movement.

Further down the track, Mr G. Hayman and Sir Tyrrell peered at a picture on the wall, faded by time and blackened by the filthy output of the steam engines. Mr G. Hayman held her lantern up to examine it more closely.

'What are they?' she asked.

'This tunnel used to be a public walkway before it was sold to the railway company,' explained Sir Tyrrell.

The scene showed Nero playing the fiddle while Rome burnt. The Roman Emperor's face was contorted into one of insane joy.

'It makes you wonder, how much these pictures do not show,' said Mr G. Hayman. 'How much of the world's history is hidden from us?'

Sir Tyrrell glanced over his shoulder at Tom's elaborate preparations. 'How long can it take?'

'You are impatient for immortality?' replied Mr G. Hayman.

'I'm impatient to know whether it is truly possible.'

'You still doubt it after what we have seen the boy do?'

'The same boy who stole the book, a street urchin of no breeding at all. How do we know he does not mean to trick us now?'

'It would not be in his interests. Lord Ringmore has promised him everything he desires, but he will get none of it if any harm comes to us. No, I believe the Eternity Spell is the book's great gift to us, Olwyn Broe's final spell.'

'But if it's possible it raises so many questions. If it has been done before it stands to reason there must be those amongst us old enough to have witnessed the scene painted onto this wall the first time around.'

'It's not such a stretch of the imagination. After all, I've seen your English politicians. I swear some of those are as old as Moses himself,' responded Mr G. Hayman, dryly.

Sir Tyrrell snorted at the joke. 'But would it not be to society's benefit for those immortals to make themselves known? Imagine the knowledge they would have amassed.'

'Perhaps society's benefit is not their goal.'

'Well, if I live forever I will take great pride in sharing the wisdom I will have gained from my experience.'

'You seek to influence the future by dwelling on the past?'

'I seek to make the world a better place. What about you? What is your reason for being here?'

'As the poet wrote, *You still shall live, such virtue hath my pen, where breath most breathes, even in the mouths of men.*' Mr G. Hayman took a couple of steps and held her lantern up to an illustration of the pyramids of Egpyt. 'I used to believe that art was the only path to immortality. It's what made me want to pick up a pen. But even if my books remain in print after I am dead, what good is it to me? What good is the point of adulation if you are not there to appreciate it?'

'It would appear that was Clay's view when he decided to split from the Society. There is hardly a soul in London not talking about his new magic show.'

'Clay's sense of self-preservation has always been his driving force. He is too wrapped up in the present to care for the future. I only hope he can control and contain the power he has unleashed.'

'And what of Ringmore?' asked Sir Tyrrell, gesticulating towards him.

'Death cheated him out of his parents,' said Mr G.

Hayman. 'He seeks the last word.'

'Ah, yes, the last word,' said Sir Tyrrell, ruefully. 'The question is, once one has conquered death, what is there left to fear?'

'Oh, there is always something to fear.'

62

Escape

Posters about Harry Clay's new magic show had sprung up across the city. Every publication had something to say about it, but it wasn't any of these things which led Esther to the Theatre Royal in Victoria. She could feel the vibrations of the magic spreading through the theatre walls. Tom was still busy with the Society of Thirteen, which meant that someone else was behind it. Waiting outside, Esther spotted Worms and Stump loitering by the stage door. There was no sign of Hardy but when Brewer emerged, with a hood pulled over his head, obscuring his face, Esther was in no doubt she had found the person responsible for Harry Clay's new success. Brewer stepped into a hansom cab with Clay, leaving Worms and Stump by the theatre. Esther ran after the cab and jumped onto the back.

The clattering of the wheels made it impossible to hear what Clay and Brewer were talking about until it drew up outside Clay's house on Millbank and they stepped out.

'You're getting careless. You could have killed me tonight,' said Clay angrily.

'I could have killed you every night,' replied Brewer, hoarsely. His face was still hidden.

The door opened and Esther crept around the side of the house to a window. A light came on and she saw Clay and Brewer step into the library. Brewer retreated to a dark corner and kept his hood up and his cloak gathered around his body.

'I don't understand what it is you want,' stated Clay. 'Have I not stood by our bargain? Have I not lived up to my side?'

'I want more,' whispered Brewer.

'You've already increased your cut threefold.'

'I want more,' he repeated.

'Now Brewer, I know you're probably thinking that without you I don't have an act, but remember, I am the face of this show.'

'Without me, all you got is tricks, the same as everyone else.'

'I could just as easily find another orphan who will be more grateful for the helping hand,' said Clay. 'Don't forget who it was that gave you this power.'

'You think I've forgotten it was you who did this to me?' Brewer threw back his hood and revealed an uneven skull with his thin hair now reduced to clumps clinging onto the sore, blistered skin, with huge, pus-filled warts everywhere. 'You see what you made me?' shouted Brewer. With the flick of a hand, he sent books flying across the room. Esther felt the ripples of his magic wash over her but it was dark and ugly.

'Your condition worsens. We must find you a doctor,' said Clay.

'No doctor can help me,' said Brewer. 'You had me draw this poison into my body and now it feasts on my flesh. I sold my soul to you, Clay.'

'I can speak to Hayman and find out more about this condition,' said Clay. 'I can help you.'

Brewer had stopped listening. He sniffed the air like an animal picking up another's scent. Esther ducked out of sight and gripped her staff tightly. She could feel him moving closer. The potent stench of lifeblood was on his breath. She began to move her staff when there was a knock on the front door.

'Who's that?' said Brewer.

'Whoever it is, you cannot be seen here,' replied Clay.

Esther moved to the corner of the house where she could see two uniformed police officers and a third man, wearing a smart suit, standing on the doorstep. All three entered the house but, when Esther looked through the window, only the smartly dressed man was led into the room by Clay's man. Brewer had turned himself invisible but Esther could tell from the waves of Conjury that he was still in the room.

'I said no visitors, Fred,' said Clay.

'Chief Inspector Longdale would like a word,' replied Fred.

'I am very sorry for this intrusion,' said Longdale.

Clay dismissed Fred and waited until he had closed the door behind him before speaking. 'How can I help you?'

'I am leading an investigation into a very serious matter. The murder of a boy known as Hardy.'

'Should the name mean something to me?' asked Clay.

'His body was found near the river, not so far from here.'

'Are you speaking to everyone in the area?'

'Not everyone,' replied Chief Inspector Longdale. 'I understand you recently visited the orphanage where this boy grew up, a place by the name of St Clement's.'

'As an orphan myself I am often looking for institutions worthy of my charity.'

'How did you find this one?'

'Lacking in compassion.'

Longdale nodded but didn't allow himself to get distracted from his line of enquiry. 'The boy Hardy also revisited this place. He was given your name by the prioress.'

'Therefore you think there must be some connection,' surmised Clay.

'Did the boy find you?' asked Longdale.

'He did.' If Clay was disconcerted by the interrogation his cool exterior gave nothing away.

'May I ask what he wanted?'

'He wanted to learn my trade. He's not the first to do so. He was looking for a way out. Sounds as though you're saying he found one.'

'What did you say to him?' asked the inspector.

'The same thing I say to all that come asking. I tell them I cannot help them.'

'You sent him away?'

'I did not reach this position by giving away my secrets. I told him to stay out of trouble and sent him packing.'

Chief Inspector Longdale removed his spectacles, pulled a handkerchief from his top pocket and cleaned the lenses. He held them up to the light to check for smears and noticed a reflection in the glass. He turned to see what it was and saw the boy standing in the middle of the room.

'Brewer?' said Longdale, unable to hide the look of disgust on his face. 'Is that you?'

'You wanted Hardy's killer?' said Brewer. 'You're looking at him.'

'Then I think you had better accompany me down the station. Both of you.' He pulled out a set of handcuffs and slapped them over Clay's wrists.

'Brewer, what are you playing at?' asked Clay. 'I had this under control.'

'Control?' Brewer laughed bitterly. 'You got no control.'

He raised his left hand and sent books flying from the shelves, raining down on Longdale's head.

'No good will come of this,' shouted Clay.

The books flew around the room, their covers flapping like wings. Longdale tried to bat them away as they continued to attack. The door rattled as the police officers tried to get in but Brewer had sealed it shut with another spell.

'Stop this now!' demanded Clay.

Brewer turned to face him and smiled.

'Brewer?' Something rattled above Clay's head. He looked up to see several nails fly out of the wall, allowing a large rusty chain to drop to the floor. The first chain from which Clay had ever escaped reared up like a huge snake and slithered towards him. With his hands still cuffed, Clay was unable to prevent it wrapping itself around him.

'Let's see you escape this time,' said Brewer.

Clay's face revealed undiluted fear. The chain was crushing his ribcage, restricting his breathing. Esther moved her staff and snapped her fingers and the links disconnected and fell to the floor. Brewer turned to look through the window. His face was even worse than before, the warts so bulbous that he could barely open his eyes. He raised his hands and sent the chain links through the window towards her. Esther raised her hand and the chain links and bits of broken glass flew harmlessly past her.

'This is none of your business, orphan,' said Brewer.

'I won't let you kill them,' replied Esther.

'And who's going to stop me killing you?' said Brewer. With another wave of his hands he ripped a bookshelf from the wall and sent two spear-like pieces of wood at her. Esther's hand was already raised in defence and the shards caught fire and burnt so fast that by the time they hit her they were nothing but blackened ash.

'Brewer, you have to find a mirror before it's too late,' said Esther.

'You want a mirror?' replied Brewer. The mirror from the wall came free and Esther prepared to protect herself but Brewer had other plans for it. He made it hover above Longdale's head. The vicious books were holding him down, preventing him from getting away from the heavy mirror.

'Why would you want to protect these pathetic souls?' asked Brewer.

'Because I can.' Esther sent the mirror out of the window, over her head and smashing against the wall behind her.

'These spells will kill you,' she warned. 'You need to stop.'

Brewer raised his hand but, as Esther braced herself, he collapsed. The lifeblood was taking its toll. The boils on his head and neck pulsated. He reached a hand to touch his face.

'What's . . . what's happening to me?' he asked.

'The Earthsoul is reclaiming its lifeblood,' said Esther.

Brewer's scream sounded like a wild animal. He tore off his shirt, revealing his blistered torso covered in throbbing boils. Longdale stood up and the two policemen finally got through the door. All three stared in astonishment at Brewer, writhing on the ground.

'Help me . . .' he begged, crawling towards the window, reaching out a hand.

Esther vanished from sight.

Brewer snarled, wriggled and kicked then, one by one, the blisters burst, releasing deep green pus from within, like volcanos erupting all over his skin. The liquid gushed over his body and dragged it down to the ground. It oozed from the open sores that covered him and stained the carpet. It dripped through the floorboards.

The other two policemen had turned away in revulsion but Chief Inspector Longdale kept his eyes on Brewer until he was no more than a mass of rotten bones and flesh.

'What is this witchery?' he whispered. 'Clay?'

There was no reply.

He turned around. 'Where is he?'

The officers shrugged. He had been there when they entered but when they searched the room, all they could find were a pair of open handcuffs.

63

Kiyaya

Esther stopped under a streetlamp and gazed out at the river, trying to find some comfort from its power, but nothing could erase from her mind the image of the lifeblood bursting out of Brewer's tortured body. She shuddered as she wondered if the same fate awaited her. When the time came, would the Infected blood that rushed through her veins return to the great underground rivers of the Earth-soul? Or would the same instinct that had caused her to perform the Creation Spell in the first place push her to choose an animal existence like that of Mondriat or Olwyn, rather than death?

When she started walking again she became aware of a presence behind her. She gripped her staff and turned around. Kiyaya stood there.

'You must come,' he said. 'Your friend needs you.'

'Tom? What's wrong?'

'He is being tricked by the magpie.'

'What's Mondriat making him do?'

'The boy is performing shaded magic far beyond his reach,' replied Kiyaya. 'He is creating a potion so complex, it will take a great deal of his spirit. He will be very weak once it's finished. I fear he may not recover at all.' Kiyaya offered his left hand. 'Come. I can take you. You must place your hand in mine.'

Esther went to take it.

'No. Your right hand,' said Kiyaya. 'It will only work if it is your right hand.'

Esther hesitated, knowing that to move her staff into the other hand would leave her vulnerable and unable to use Conjury to defend herself.

'Quickly. There is not much time,' said the Indian.

'How do I know I can trust you?'

'We are beyond the point of trusting now,' he replied simply.

Esther moved her staff into her left hand and took his. His skin was soft and warm. She watched him move his staff slowly. As he brought it heavily down on the ground, it was as though he was smashing a mirror, except that it was not glass that broke but the world around them. They fell like shards of glass.

64

Completion

As Tom worked away on the spell, Mondriat fluttered around the tunnel with the book in his beak, so that Tom could see the picture. Mondriat could see the boy was getting tired, but he was so close now.

'There are only three strokes left,' said Mondriat, dropping the book from his beak as he spoke.

'What strokes?' panted Tom.

'This spell has a triangular cauldron at its heart,' said Mondriat. 'It draws on deeply shaded magic.'

Tom drew the final three lines and created a large cauldron in the tunnel floor. Finally, he lowered his staff, exhausted.

'Well done, Tom.' Mondriat clapped his wings, excitedly. 'Masterfully done.'

Sir Tyrrell and Mr G. Hayman gathered around Lord Ringmore, who had barely blinked since Tom had begun.

'Is it done?' asked Sir Tyrrell.

'Of course it's not done, you old fool,' snapped Mondriat.

'Wait.' Tom held up his hand, head bowed, too tired to say any more. Slowly he rolled up his shirt sleeve and held an arm over the centre of the cauldron. Mondriat fluttered up and landed on his arm.

'You are weak from the rigours of the spell,' said Mondriat. 'The loss of blood will weaken you further.'

'Do it,' said Tom.

'Very well.' Mondriat jabbed his beak into the soft skin of his palm and Tom closed his fist around the broken skin before allowing a couple of drops to fall.

'What is this black magic that calls for the boy's blood?' demanded Sir Tyrrell.

'It is a potion,' whispered Mr G. Hayman.

The Society members watched in silent astonishment as Tom's blood sunk into the ground and the red liquid oozed out of the earth's pores, filling up the cauldron.

'It's ready.' Tom staggered back and would have fallen had Lord Ringmore not been there to catch him.

'What's wrong with him?' asked Sir Tyrrell.

'This is powerful magic, you half-witted buffoon,' said Mondriat. 'Creating a spell such as this would take its toll on the most experienced Conjuror.'

Even though Lord Ringmore could not understand Mondriat's words, he could see Tom needed rest so he dragged him to the side of the tunnel and placed him down gently before joining the others.

'I can't see,' said Tom.

'Your senses will recover,' said Mondriat.

'What are they doing?' Tom asked.

'Preparing to drink,' replied the magpie. 'And look, they even remembered to bring glasses.'

Sir Tyrrell opened a case and pulled out three silver goblets, one for each of the Society members.

Mr G. Hayman held up one to inspect it. 'These are rather grand, aren't they?'

'They were sold to me by one who swore them exact replicas of the Holy Grail itself,' said Sir Tyrrell. 'I thought they would be appropriate for an occasion such as this.'

'I daresay the price reflected the boldness of the claim,' said Mr G. Hayman.

'They are fine pieces and should do well for our purposes,' said Lord Ringmore, keen get on with it.

'They stoop to fill their cups now,' said Mondriat, excitedly.

'How should we do this?' asked Sir Tyrrell.

'As one,' said Lord Ringmore. 'We are in this together.'

'Should someone say something?' asked Sir Tyrrell, holding his cup in both hands. 'You know, to mark the occasion.'

'Honestly,' remarked Mondriat impatiently. 'Even a short time with these fools would feel like an eternity.'

'I think a simple toast,' said Lord Ringmore.

'To the Society of Thirteen?' asked Mr G. Hayman.

'To the rest of our lives,' stated Lord Ringmore.

The others repeated the toast and touched goblets before downing the contents.

'They're drinking . . . they're drinking,' said Mondriat, but Tom was too weak to respond.

With their goblets drained, the Society members looked at each other uncertainly. Mondriat hopped up and down on Tom's shoulder.

'Is that it then?' asked Sir Tyrrell. 'Are we immortal?'

'I don't feel any different,' said Mr G. Hayman.

'I feel rather lightheaded,' said Sir Tyrrell.

'What's happening?' asked Tom weakly.

'The lifeblood is within them,' said Mondriat, watching with great interest. Never having seen this potion before he was also keen to know what would happen.

'My eyes,' said Sir Tyrrell. 'My sight has gone.'

'Mine too,' said Lord Ringmore.

'The lifeblood has blinded us so that we may see the true nature of the world,' said Mr G. Hayman.

'Hold on, I see something,' said Sir Tyrrell. 'It is London, but it burns. Fires rage everywhere. People run through the streets, pillaging and looting like invaders and yet these are the city's very inhabitants.'

'My vision is unlike yours,' said Mr G. Hayman. 'I see a girl in a graveyard. Is this the future, the past? What?'

'What about you, Ringmore? What can you see?' asked Sir Tyrrell.

'Father,' said Lord Ringmore. 'I see my father. He is young again.'

'The past, present and future are as one within the Earth-soul,' said Mondriat.

'What does this mean?' demanded Sir Tyrrell.

Mondriat became aware of the black cat by his side. He turned to see her bright green eyes watching intently.

'Olwyn. Something has gone wrong,' he said.

'Not at all,' replied Olwyn. 'They are looking directly into the Earthsoul. Their spirits are being torn from their bodies.'

Suddenly all three dropped to the ground, heaving and retching as though about to vomit.

'Help me . . .' cried Lord Ringmore, reaching out a hand, his eyes wide with fear.

His words were lost as he and the other Society members opened their mouths, but it was not the contents of their stomachs that spilt out. It was the white light of three human spirits evacuating their helpless bodies. The spirits sunk into the ground, leaving behind the three bodies, empty and lifeless.

65

Preservation

Tom was lost inside the shifting clouds that filled his head. The fog swam through his brain as Mondriat's laughter echoed off the tunnel walls.

'Olwyn, you clever, clever Conjuress, you,' proclaimed Mondriat.

'So you understand, do you?' said the female voice.

'Understand what?' yelled Tom.

'Calm yourself,' urged Mondriat. 'You knew this would happen, didn't you, Olwyn?'

'It's the only way to get that which we desire,' replied Olwyn.

'What's happened to Ringmore and the others?' shouted Tom.

'The Society of Thirteen is no more,' said Mondriat.

'And yet they will rise again,' purred Olwyn.

'Well, two of them, at least,' added Mondriat, bursting with excitement.

It was too much for Tom to take in. He felt exhausted and distanced by the clouds in his mind.

'So, let's see,' said Mondriat. 'The potion purified their spirits, drawing them down into the heart of the Earthsoul without harming the bodies.'

'You've killed them,' said Tom.

'No. They chose to drink and their spirits will now live forever within the Earthsoul,' said Olwyn.

'Why?' shouted Tom. 'Why have you done this?'

'Is it not obvious?' said Mondriat. 'These bodies are perfectly preserved. So let us say we know a pair of Conjurors in search of new bodies; there would be nothing to stop them from slipping inside one of these fine specimens. There would be nothing to prevent them from returning to human form. Oh, Olwyn, you glorious Conjuress.'

'I was thinking Lord Ringmore would suit you best,' she replied. 'The politician, as powerful as he is, carries too much weight with too weak a heart. I'll take the female, of course. I don't think I'm quite ready for male anatomy.'

'So you knew all along. Why did you not tell me?' said Mondriat.

'Because I enjoy toying with you, my dear,' said Olwyn. 'I always did.'

'But this is marvellous. We can return, you and I. We can be as we were before.'

Tom's head swam with confusion. In amongst the shifting shapes of the fog he tried to make sense of it all. There were strange sounds and a light so bright that it even shone through the fog in his mind. When Mondriat and Olwyn next spoke their voices had changed. They now used the vocal chords of Lord Ringmore and Mr G. Hayman.

'I'm back,' cried Mondriat. 'I'm back and it's all thanks to you, my wonderful Conjuress, Olwyn.'

'My darling husband,' replied Olwyn.

66

Vanquishing

When the broken fragments of the world reformed, Esther found herself standing in a tunnel in front of Lord Ringmore and Mr G. Hayman. Sir Tyrrell's unconscious body was lying on a train track. To the side sat Tom. He looked lost and bewildered. Esther tried to run to him but Kiyaya held her hand tightly and prevented her from moving.

'Please,' she begged.

'Esther?' shouted Tom, hearing her voice. 'Esther?'

'Tom!' she called.

Kiyaya did not look at her, instead addressing Mr G. Hayman. 'I have her for you,' he said. When Mr G. Hayman turned, Esther could see there was something odd about her. Lord Ringmore looked different too. Esther spotted the lifeless magpie and cat by Sir Tyrrell's body. Lord Ringmore moved his stick across the ground, and the lamplights lifted into the air.

'Mondriat?' asked Esther.

'Indeed. 'Tis I,' Lord Ringmore's body replied. He turned to Mr G. Hayman. 'This is wonderful, Olwyn, wonderful.'

'I can't tell you how much it pleases me to see you so happy,' replied Olwyn, in the body of Mr G. Hayman.

'And it pleases me to see you so exquisitely, deliciously . . . . human,' replied Mondriat. The lamps grew brighter. 'You planned this whole thing, didn't you? Everything from the beginning.'

'All for you.' Olwyn smiled.

Mondriat sent the lanterns spinning around. 'The book was the bait,' he said. 'Tom was the fisherman and these splendidly wealthy, unInfected people were your fish. I have so missed all this.' Mondriat slipped an arm around her waist. 'But why didn't you tell me?'

'I wanted it to be a surprise, my love,' said Olwyn. She tenderly stroked the side of Mondriat's face with the back of her hand.

'And all that stuff about you not trusting me?'

'Never confuse trust with love.'

'You've killed them,' exclaimed Esther, horrified.

'They have purified these bodies and now they wear their scalps,' said Kiyaya.

Mondriat turned to face the huge man. 'And I see we have another Conjuror amongst us. How this mystery deepens,' said Mondriat. 'I take it this has something to do with you, Olwyn.'

'He is no ordinary Conjuror, are you, Kiyaya?' replied Olwyn.

'I have walked in many forms,' he replied.

'An old soul,' said Mondriat with wonder. 'I feel like such a fool. Olwyn, you always could make a fool of me.'

Olwyn reached out her right hand. 'Now please my love, I wonder if I could borrow this staff for a moment. It has been so long since I felt its power.'

Mondriat handed her Lord Ringmore's stick. 'You know I'd do anything to watch you Conjure again.'

Olwyn inspected the walking stick then moved it in a series of elegant shapes across the ground. The lamplights sparkled and fizzled with energy.

'Always such beautiful Conjury.' Mondriat sighed. 'But if you discovered all this back then, why did it take so long to use it? Why have you waited all this time? What were the complications you spoke of?'

Olwyn continued to move the staff while she answered. 'As you know, an animal's spirit may be pushed aside and its body manipulated by a Conjuror, but a human's body is more complex, more intricate. The potion separates the body without harming it but one cannot control such complex machinery while a part of oneself resides elsewhere. It takes a complete spirit to control a human form.'

'You are talking about our True Reflections?' said Mondriat.

'Yes. That which anchors us to this world is precisely that which prevents human immortality. While an image of you remains in your True Reflection, you cannot take on a new human form. No man can have more than one reflection. Is that not so, Kiyaya?'

'Where I am from we have no Mirror Spell,' responded

the Indian. 'Here in your cold continent you Conjurors were vain. You wanted to hang onto your birth skins. Where I am from, the Infected shed these skins and find new forms as early as possible. Removed from the body which cast the Creation Spell, our second skins are protected from the pull of the Earthsoul.'

As he spoke Esther felt herself transported back again to the night beneath the stars in the wilderness. She saw the man with the painted face, clutching his staff. He looked exhausted. She noticed the patterns on the ground beneath the bodies of Kiyaya's murdered family.

'The man who showed me how to Conjure also taught me how it was possible to step from body to body, never dying,' said Kiyaya. 'He only asked for one thing in exchange for his knowledge: a sacrifice. My family. That night I convinced them to drink and he took my uncle's skin while I took the hide of my cousin. It was the first of many hides I was to wear over the years.'

Esther returned to the tunnel with a jolt and saw the spell scratched on the ground around the train tracks. It was the same one as she had seen in the vision. She tried to wriggle free but Kiyaya's grip was strong.

'Then we must get to our mirrors and extract our True Reflection,' said Mondriat. 'How long do we have?'

'That depends,' replied Olwyn calmly. 'It could be minutes, hours, maybe longer. Can't you already feel the itch of Lord Ringmore's body, trying to reject your incomplete spirit?'

A panicked expression appeared on the face of Lord

Ringmore as Mondriat realised Olwyn was speaking the truth.

'Let me have the staff,' said Mondriat. 'I can get myself there at once.'

'Ah,' replied Olwyn. With a small flick of her wrist, she made Sir Tyrrell's cold hand came to life and grip Mondriat's leg.

'My love?' said Mondriat, eyes wide with fear and confusion.

Olwyn smiled. 'Always so untrustworthy and yet yourself so trusting. You even trusted me when I planted the idea in your head that mirror theft held the secret of immortality. I always knew it wouldn't work but it helped cleanse a world so overpopulated by Conjurors.'

'That was not my purpose.'

'Yet it was mine. There were too many Infected souls. It was time for an overhaul. When power becomes too commonplace it ceases to be power. You see, you were right. I am always playing games and you, Mondriat, are always my unwitting pawn.'

'I don't understand.'

'I wouldn't expect you to, but I did always enjoy watching you scrabble around desperately for the answer, so I will give you a chance. If you can reach your reflection across the streets of London with an overweight politician's body attached to your leg then you have earned your right to this human form. Perhaps you'll be able to find something to use as a staff. If not you had better hope you can find some other animal skin to take refuge in.' She stood on the magpie's neck and snapped it, then did the same to the cat. 'I think a rat might suit you next. There must be plenty of those around.'

'Please, Olwyn . . .' Mondriat tried hopelessly to prize Sir Tyrrell's fingers from his leg.

'You can waste your time here or you can get moving,' she said coolly.

He looked up at her and saw the look of unswerving determination in her eyes. 'Always such a fascinating woman,' he said wistfully. 'Olwyn, I will pass your test and return to you.'

Mondriat began making his way down the tunnel, as fast as he could while dragging Sir Tyrrell's ungainly dead body along the railway track.

'Let him go,' protested Esther.

Olwyn turned to face her. Although Olwyn no longer wore the cat's skin, there was still something feline about the way she prowled towards Esther.

'Now, Esther, I think it is time you learnt the truth too. You see, I look at you and I see myself.'

Olwyn laughed. Esther had heard that laughter somewhere before. It was the same laughter as that of the dark-haired woman she had seen inside her mirror. 'I don't know what you mean.'

'I must extract my True Reflection in order to become immortal. That's why I needed Kiyaya to bring you here.'

'What has that to do with me?'

'All this time, dear Esther, it was you. You were my mirror, all this time.'

With her right hand, Olwyn sketched out a spell. She placed her left on Esther's forehead, pushing her back into the mist of memory.

Here in the past, a dark-haired woman stands over Esther. It is Olwyn. They are in a small, sparsely furnished cottage. It is dark outside. On the floor lies a fair-haired woman. Unmoving. Esther knows this is her mother from the screaming agony her infant mind feels when she looks at her. This memory, tucked so deep inside her for so long, stretches back to a time before she had the power of speech. Olwyn crouches down beside Esther's mother, as a creature might inspect its prey. The bright light of her spirit spews out of her mouth and the dark-haired woman's body drops to the ground. Esther's mother blinks and stands, and yet it is not her mother. It is Olwyn in her body. She picks up her book and staff. Outside, fists pound on the door. Angry voices shout through the window. Torches burn. The woman throws her head back and laughs. But the laughter turns to a cough. She splutters and wretches as the body rejects her. Her spirit spills out once more and seeks refuge in her original body. Confused and scared, Esther crawls to her mother. Olwyn has the staff again. The screaming and pounding grows louder. Olwyn points her left hand at Esther's mother. Esther closes her eyes. Then all is gone.

Back in the tunnel, Olwyn released Esther. She stumbled backwards, as she was finally released by Kiyaya. She felt strange, as though something inside her had been removed. She landed hard on the ground. 'You killed her,' she said. 'You killed my mother.'

'If you're going to weep for a woman who died centuries ago there are plenty more,' replied Olwyn.

'Who was she?' demanded Esther.

'As I said before, she was no one,' said Olwyn, dismissively. 'She was the most ordinary peasant girl that ever lived. She only became relevant when I chose her.'

'Why her?'

'Because she was foolish enough and desperate enough to believe a Conjuress when she told her she could make a potion that would bring her untold wealth and happiness. She was nothing more than an unInfected fool who believed that there was an easy solution to the suffering of life and that she deserved it. Vanity and idiocy killed your mother. Not I.'

'Her body rejected you,' said Esther. 'Your spirit was incomplete.'

'Because of you.'

'What could I have done? I was a child.'

'I drew out my True Reflection from my mirror before entering the new host body. It should have worked. It took me a long time to understand what had happened. When I drew it out, it retreated to another's reflection. A child was watching. The reflection of your eye stole my True Reflection. I knew I had to hide the evidence from the barbaric hoards so I sent your mother's body where no one would look, into the folds of time. Unfortunately, in my hurry, I failed to see the book in her hand or the orphaned child weeping on her chest. By the time I realised the truth, it was too late.'

'So you had to wait all this time before you could draw

your True Reflection from within me?' said Esther.

'Yes. I waited and waited, carefully considering how, this time, I would return, but in something better than the body of some peasant girl. I'll always be grateful for Mother Agnes for taking you in, despite all that talk of the devil being inside you. She didn't know how right she was, did she, Esther?'

Esther stared back in horror at the bewitched body of Mr G. Hayman. This, she realised, was the truth. Her mother had been murdered and Esther had grown up with the True Reflection of her murderer inside of her. Strangest of all, now that Olwyn had reclaimed her True Reflection, Esther felt its loss. She felt alone. She felt empty.

67

Locomotion

As Tom's vision returned he could make out Mondriat staggering over the sleepers. Closer by, Olwyn and Kiyaya were standing in front of Esther. Tom wanted to go to her but he wasn't strong enough to get up.

'Kiyaya, why are you helping this witch?' asked Esther.

'In my land, the Infected are mistrusted,' replied the huge man. 'We are feared. We are cast out. Here, they have been gone so long, they have become myths. A living myth is a powerful thing. That is why I travelled across the ocean. Once here, the book's power drew me to it, just as it did the magpie. I wanted to find out more about the object. Luckily the unInfected are easily manipulated. I needed John Symmonds to join the Society so I made sure he and Lord Ringmore crossed paths, but when he ceased to be useful I stopped his heart and watched him die.'

'You killed him? You murdered an innocent man. Why? Why?' Esther felt sick with fear and anger.

'When you have lived as many lives as I, you accept death more readily,' replied Kiyaya. 'I no longer needed Mr Symmonds. I had met Olwyn Broe. She would help achieve that which I desired.'

'What is it you want? What could she do for you?'

'The Infected should walk tall, not cower in caves. I have lived in exile too long. Now is our time to rule.'

'So why involve me and Tom?' asked Esther. 'Why didn't you perform the Eternity Spell yourself?'

'It is one thing to create the potion,' said Kiyaya, 'you must also have someone to drink it.'

'And I needed the right body this time,' said Olwyn. 'This novelist is ideal. She can move around with the same freedom and respect as a man. She has independent means and powerful friends. She has respect. In this body I will ensure the Infected return to their rightful place.'

'Are you saying you controlled everything from the beginning?' asked Esther. 'Tom, Mondriat, Ringmore; it was all part of your game.'

'Controlled?' Olwyn considered the word. 'No. I *guided*. The book was never going to be discovered sitting in that shop, so I burnt it down. When it fell into Lord Ringmore's hands and he formed his Society, I knew I had found my targets, but my influence would have to be a subtle one. The best puppets are the ones that believe they pull their own strings.'

'But me and Tom met Ringmore by chance.'

'My True Reflection was always inside you,' said Olwyn. 'Did you not sometimes find yourself doing things that surprised you? The day you left the orphanage, the day you travelled west and targeted Lord Ringmore, the day you performed the Creation Spell. My influence on the others was subtle but you, sweet girl, I was always your guardian angel, moving you like a marionette.'

'Guardian angels don't deceive. They don't lie. They don't murder.'

'Esther,' whispered Olwyn, reaching out to touch her arm. 'I am telling you this now so you can see that I intend no further deceit. We are sisters of the lifeblood. You were my mirror for many years. Stay with me and together our power will know no limits.'

'Esther doesn't care about power,' said Tom. He had finally found the strength to get up and stagger across to take his place beside her.

'You care about power though, don't you, Tom?' said Olwyn. 'You have proved yourself a powerful Conjuror this evening.'

Tom looked at her then back at Esther. 'Not any more, I don't,' he said.

'Don't be foolish, child,' said Olwyn. 'You were happy to throw your lot in with Lord Ringmore in exchange for power. I can offer you so much more.'

'I won't kill for it,' stated Tom. 'I know what's right and what's wrong. All I care about is Esther and me. That's all that matters.'

Esther looked at him and saw finally that she had the old Tom back. The Tom who had left the orphanage with her in search of something better. The Tom who had followed her through the streets of London as they learnt how to survive. The Tom who was the only family she had ever known. Her friend, Tom.

'How touching,' said Olwyn. 'But since you will not join me, I will dispose of you both.' She moved her staff and raised her left hand.

The orphans heard the rumbling approach of a train behind them.

'If I am to start afresh in this guise, these deaths must be explained away,' said Olwyn. 'No one will understand why Sir Tyrrell, Lord Ringmore and a pair of orphans came down this tunnel, but when they are ploughed down by an unscheduled train, there will be no question about what killed them.'

The rumbling grew louder as the train thundered towards them. Esther raised her hand and tried to stop it but the train continued to roll in their direction. She tried to pull it apart but could feel Olwyn's strength in its turning wheels and its pumping pistons. Her powerful Conjury held every nut and bolt in place. As the train came into sight, Esther could see, on the front, the face of the dark-haired woman.

'You cannot prevent this,' shouted Olwyn over the sound of the approaching train. 'I am a vastly more experienced Conjuress. Whatever spell you try, I will counteract it. Neither of you can escape this death. It is your fate.'

Esther felt her hands shake as she struggled against her. Olwyn was too strong. Tom raised his hands too but neither could stop the approach of the train. Sparks flew off the wheels and the screeching noise reverberated off the walls.

Tom spun around and sent the oil lamps flying at Olwyn, but Kiyaya made them fall to the ground. Tom drew the tiles from the walls, bringing them down upon Kiyaya's head, but with a tap from his great staff he vanished time and again, avoiding every attack.

'Olwyn! Please, no,' cried Mondriat in the distance.

Steam filled the tunnel.

Everything was lost in darkness.

Esther felt Tom's shoulder against her own. This wasn't how it was supposed to end. All her life Esther had felt as though there was something guiding her but it hadn't been fate as she had thought. It had nothing to do with God or providence. Nothing was pre-written. She was in control of her own actions. She could decide what to do herself. Finally, the thoughts in her head were her own. Finally, she would make her own decisions. The right decisions. Esther took Tom's left hand in hers and looked into his eyes.

'I won't let her succeed,' she said. 'Not after all she has done.'

'Then what?'

'Do you trust me?'

'Always.'

Holding his hand, they both moved in a circle, dragging their staffs on the ground, drawing out power. They could not stop the train, nor escape, but they no longer cared about that. They could feel the power of the Earthsoul all around them, its eternal strength keeping them safe. Esther could see into Tom's mind and he into hers. The orphans raised their hands and, with the smallest of movements, brought the walls crashing in on them.

The water that gushed into the tunnel wiped out everything in its path: the train, Olwyn, Kiyaya, Mondriat and Sir Tyrrell. All were caught in its ferocity. Tom squeezed Esther's hand tightly and, in place of the rushing violence of the water, was a vision: a memory.

Five years old, Tom sat in a corner, crying. The other orphans ignored him. The nuns had no words of comfort. He was all alone. He was sobbing because his aunt had left him and his mother was dead and if there was ever any hope, it was not here in this place. He had never felt such unending sadness, when a girl appeared. She was the same age as him but confident and with eyes that shone like pennies in the dirt.

'Hello,' she said. 'There's no need to cry. It will be all right.'

Tom turned away and continued to sob.

'I'll be your friend if you like,' she said. 'My name is Esther.'

Tom looked up at her. He stopped crying and smiled.

Epilogue

Amy knows she should go home. It is cold. It is late. The miserable soaps finished ages ago. She has been out too long. Her grandparents will have noticed she isn't in her bedroom. Perhaps they will call the police. Perhaps they will call the lady who comes on Wednesdays. Amy tries to remember if she's told her about the cemetery.

The cemetery reveals different things at night. When Amy moves the torch up her favourite gravestone she notices something she has never seen before. The shadows of the torchlight reveal a shape above the name. Carved into the stone is a circle inside a triangle inside a larger circle. Amy runs her fingertips over it. She swings the torch around to the other two gravestones and sees that the same shape is on them too. How has she never noticed it before? She wonders what it means.

Voices call her name.

'Amy? Amy?'

'Are you out there, love?'

'You're not in trouble, Amy. Just answer us, please.'

The voices belong to her grandparents and to other people.

She thinks the lady who comes on Wednesdays is one of them. A blue police light flashes through the trees. Amy is about to call out when she hears a tapping.

She turns. Sitting on top of Lord Ringmore's gravestone is a magpie. Its feathers are tattered and ruffled. She has never seen a bird like it. It reminds her of something but she's not sure what. It taps the gravestone with its beak. It taps the shape above Lord Ringmore's name. The circle within a triangle within a circle.

Amy looks down at the stick she picked up to protect herself. The bird flutters down to the ground and she understands what it wants. It wants her to draw the shape in the ground. She doesn't know how she understands this but she is sure this is what it means. Carefully, she does so.

'Amy . . . Amy . . .'

The voices are growing nearer.

The bird taps the middle of the shape on the gravestone. Amy understands. She steps into the centre of the shape and feels a sudden rush. She is dizzy and yet everything is clearer than it has ever been. She hears every rustle of every leaf in the cemetery. She can see her grandparents and the others, even though they cannot see her. The lady who comes on Wednesdays is with them. They don't look as angry as she expected. Amy wishes they would go away. She opens her eyes. She didn't even realise they had been shut. She looks at the bird.

'So?' says the magpie. 'Would you like to disappear, then?'

Q & A with Gareth P. Jones

Where did the idea for The Society of Thirteen *come from?*

I've always wanted to write a book involving magic, but I needed it to be a magic I could believe in. Last year, I was up in Chester for a book festival when I wandered into a museum and saw a notice about a local history group called The Society of Thirteen (named so because of the number of people who formed it, I believe). I really liked the name so I jotted it down in my ideas book. It remained there for a while until I looked at it out of context and got thinking about how thirteen is an unlucky number. It occurred to me that there was a direct link between superstitions and stories of magic. They all have their roots in folklore, and there is lots of overlap. When I had made that connection, I realised that I'd found my way into magic. If I began with the idea that every superstition had some basis in the reality of magic, it would help ground my magic and make it something I could believe in. It became a very earthy magic, not something that could be bought in a magical shop, but rather something very natural. Once I began to see how it would work I realised that it wouldn't be something that would yield to anything as modern as language. My spells wouldn't be spoken while waving a flimsy wand. They would be drawn out of the earth.

Where did the word 'Conjury' come from?

Having worked out the mechanics of my magic, I had to decide on the lexicon. Would I be writing about wizards, witches, warlocks, magicians or something else? Would they have wands, staffs or broomsticks? The solutions to these questions came from some background reading. While looking into stories of magic I came across the idea of *Cunning Men*. These were folk healers, generally considered less threatening than witches, due to their usefulness. As my story developed, I realised that there would be an element of non-magical trickery and misdirection. I began to see a link between cunning men, conning men and conjurors. That's when it became apparent my wizards would be known as conjurors. The more I thought about it the more I liked the idea that one could literally conjure up power from the earth.

Why did you choose the term the 'Infected'?

I knew very early on that gaining magical powers was going to involve some sacrifice. Given the orphans' Catholic upbringing, it felt right that there would be an element of selling one's soul in order to obtain such power. After all, if thirteen is the age one must be to discover magic then there must be a reason that has been remembered as an unlucky number. Of course, once you've established that terrible things will happen to those who don't perform the Mirror Spell, it would be disappointing not to see them.

How much research did you do for the book?

As usual, not as much as I'd have liked. I'm sure a good pedant could find lots of historical inaccuracies. I have taken various liberties with my London of 1891. The Theatre Royal, where Clay performs, would actually have been called Royal Standard Music Hall, although I did retain the real name of the proprietor, Mr Dickey. There was no flood in the tunnel under the Thames in 1891 either. More important than details like these is the evocation of a world that seems convincingly like late Victorian London. I relied on the same resources I used when writing *Constable & Toop*, but I also read a book about the relationship between Sir Arthur Conan Doyle and Harry Houdini, elements of which dripped into the characters Lord Ringmore, Harry Clay and Mr G. Hayman.

What is the purpose of the epilogue and prologue in this book?

When I started, I thought Amy's story was going to be a much bigger part and run alongside the Victorian action but, as I wrote, the Victorian elements elbowed their way to the front, while Amy's story got pushed to the sides. That means there is a danger that some readers will consider those two chapters irrelevant and distracting. I hope not. I left them in for a reason. There are several points where characters think about the connection between story and history. This is one of the themes of the book. Amy creates her own stories from the snapshots of the past she finds on the gravestones. This is precisely what I do when I wander through cemeteries stealing names from gravestones and using them in my stories. Who knows if Amy's (or mine) are any more fantastical than the real lives of the real people?

Do you wander through cemeteries, stealing names from gravestones a lot?

Quite a lot, yes.

As with your previous books, this one delves into the darker aspects of life. Do you think subjects such as murder, death and disease are suitable for children's literature?

I do. I think children spend a lot of time making sense of all these things, and literature should not shy away from addressing them. It's only ever the adults I worry about when I do public readings. They're much more scared of this stuff than my usual readership.

Religion doesn't come out very well in this book . . .

I don't think that's true. Mother Agnes abuses her position. She is sadistic and mean and has nothing to do with what Christianity is supposed to be about. I intentionally made sure that Inspector Longdale had a more Christian approach to life. In an earlier draft, John Symmonds also demonstrated these qualities but then, unfortunately, he went and got himself killed.

Do you believe in magic?

No.

Finally, is it true you always write a song about each of your books and, if so, have you written the one for this book?

Yes and yes. I have finally got it in a shape I'm happy with. One of the biggest challenges with new songs is coming up with an interactive element that is different to my other songs, but, as I say, I think I have it now. The song is called *Thirteen is Unlucky for Some.*

Gareth P. Jones

Gareth spends most of his time writing. When he's not doing that he has been known to produce the occasional TV programme. He lives with his wife (Lisa), son (Herbie) and a lot of musical instruments. He won the Blue Peter Book of the Year Prize 2012 for THE CONSIDINE CURSE. THE CASE OF THE MISSING CATS, the first book in The Dragon Detective Agency series, was nominated for the Waterstones Children's Book Prize. THE THORNTHWAITE INHERITANCE won the Hounslow Junior Book Award, the Calderdale Book Award, Leicester Children's Book Award, Sefton Super Reads, Doncaster Book Award, Rotherham Children's Book Award, and Fantastic Book Award, Lancaster. He writes songs inspired by his books, which he plays on a ukulele when he visits schools.

Follow Gareth at www.garethwrites.co.uk or on Twitter: @jonesgarethp

Discover more at hotkeybooks.com!

Now you've finished, why not delve into a whole new world of books online?

- Find out more about the author, and ask them that question you can't stop thinking about!
- Get recommendations for other brilliant books – you can even download excerpts and extra content!
- Make a reading list, or browse ours for inspiration – and look out for special guests' reading lists too…
- Follow our blog and sign up to our newsletter for sneak peeks into future Hot Key releases, tips for aspiring writers and exclusive cover reveals.
- Talk to us! We'd love to hear what you thought about the book.

And don't forget you can also find us online on Twitter, Facebook, Instagram, Pinterest and YouTube! Just search for Hot Key Books